The baby.

She was still crying, and even though the sound was muffled, it was enough for Landon to pinpoint their location. Tessa was headed for the back exit.

And then he saw her.

Tessa saw him, too.

She didn't stop. With the baby gripped in her arms, she threw open the glass door and was within a heartbeat of getting outside to the parking lot. She might have made it, too, but Landon took hold of her arms and pulled her back inside.

As he'd done by the barn, he was as gentle with her as he could be, but he wasn't feeling very much of that gentleness inside.

"Please, just let me go." Her eyes filled with tears. "It's not safe for you to be with me."

"What the hell does that mean?" Landon snapped.

She closed her eyes, the tears spilling down her cheeks. "I'm not who you think I am. And if you stay here with me, they'll kill you."

LANDON

USA TODAY Bestselling Author

DELORES FOSSEN

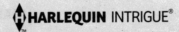

Recycling programs
for this product may
not exist in your area.

ISBN-13: 978-0-373-69938-4

Landon

Copyright © 2016 by Delores Fossen

Printed in U.S.A.

Delores Fossen, a *USA TODAY* bestselling author, has sold over fifty novels with millions of copies of her books in print worldwide. She's received a Booksellers' Best Award and an RT Reviewers' Choice Best Book Award. She was also a finalist for a prestigious RITA® Award. You can contact the author through her website at deloresfossen.com.

Books by Delores Fossen

Harlequin Intrigue

The Lawmen of Silver Creek Ranch

Grayson
Dade
Nate
Kade
Gage
Mason
Josh
Sawyer
Landon

Appaloosa Pass Ranch

Lone Wolf Lawman
Taking Aim at the Sheriff
Trouble with a Badge
The Marshal's Justice
Six-Gun Showdown
Laying Down the Law

HQN Books

The McCord Brothers

Texas on My Mind
Lone Star Nights
Blame It on the Cowboy

Visit the Author Profile page at Harlequin.com for more titles.

CAST OF CHARACTERS

Deputy Landon Ryland—A cowboy cop on a quest to find a killer. He didn't expect his old flame to show up in town with a newborn in her arms and no memory of who she is and why someone is after her.

Tessa Sinclair—After she's attacked and left for dead, Tessa has gaps in her memory, and those gaps could be shielding a killer from the law. She doesn't want to turn to Landon, but she has no choice.

Samantha—The newborn at the center of the danger. But whose child is she?

Ward Strickland—A Justice Department agent who could be on the take, but he claims he only wants to help Tessa.

Quincy Nagel—Years ago Landon sent him to prison, but now that he's a free man, Quincy could be looking for revenge.

Courtney Hager—Tessa's friend who's on the run, but she also has a lot of secrets.

Joel Mercer—A businessman with plenty of shady ties. One of those ties is possibly to Agent Ward Strickland.

Sheriff Grayson Ryland—He's the top lawman at Silver Creek Ranch, and he wants to put a quick end to the danger.

Chapter One

Deputy Landon Ryland was looking for a killer.

He stood back from the crowd who'd gathered for the graveside funeral, and Landon looked at each face of the fifty or so people. Most he'd known since he was a kid, when he had visited his Ryland cousins here in Silver Creek, Texas.

But today he had to consider that one of them might have murdered Emmett.

Just the thought of it felt as if someone had Landon's heart in a vise and was crushing it. Emmett and he were cousins. But more like brothers. And now Emmett was dead, and someone was going to pay for that.

Especially considering how, and why, Emmett had died.

Landon knew the how, but it was the why that was causing his sleepless nights. He intended to give the killer a whole lot worse than just lack of sleep, though.

He glanced out of the corner of his eye when he sensed someone approaching. Landon didn't exactly have a welcoming expression, and everybody had kept their distance. So far.

Since he was on edge, he slid his hand over his gun, but it wasn't necessary. It was Sheriff Grayson Ryland, yet another of his cousins.

Grayson, however, was also Landon's new boss.

The ink was barely dry on his contract with the sheriff's office, but he was the newest lawman in Silver Creek. Newest resident, too, of the Silver Creek Ranch since he'd moved to the guesthouse there until he could find his own place. Landon just wished his homecoming had been under much better circumstances.

"You see anything?" Grayson said. He was tall, lanky and in charge merely by being there. Grayson didn't just wear a badge—he was the law in Silver Creek, and everybody knew it.

Grayson was no doubt asking if Landon had seen a killer. He hadn't. But one thing was for certain: *she* wasn't here.

"Any sign of her yet?" Landon asked.

Grayson shook his head, but like Landon, he continued to study the funeral attendees, looking at each one of them from beneath the brim of his cowboy hat. Also as Landon had done, Grayson lingered a moment on Emmett's three brothers. All grief stricken. And that didn't apply just to them but to the entire Ryland clan. Losing one of their own had cut them each to the bone.

"Tessa Sinclair might not be able to attend, because she could be dead," Grayson reminded him.

Yes. She could be. But unless Landon found proof of that, she was a person of interest in Emmett's death. Or at least, that was how Grayson had labeled her. To Landon, she was a suspect for accessory to murder since Emmett's body had been found in her house. That meant she likely knew the killer.

She could even be protecting him.

Well, she wouldn't protect that piece of dirt once Landon found him. And old times wouldn't play into this. It didn't matter that once she'd been Landon's lover. Didn't matter that once they'd had feelings for each other.

Something that didn't sit well with him, either.

But despite how Landon felt about her and no matter how hard he looked at the attendees, Tessa wasn't here at the funeral. With her blond hair and starlet looks, she would stick out, and Landon would have already spotted her.

Grayson reached in his pocket, pulled out a silver star badge and handed it to Landon. It caught the sunlight just right, and the glare cut across Landon's face, forcing him to shut his eyes for a second. He hoped that wasn't some kind of bad sign.

"You're certain you really want this?" Grayson pressed.

"Positive." He glanced at his cousin. Not quite like looking in a mirror but close enough. The Ryland genes were definitely the dominant ones in both of them. "You haven't changed your mind about hiring me, have you?"

"Nope. I can use the help now that I'm short a

deputy. I just want to make sure you know what you're getting into."

Landon knew. He was putting himself in a position to catch a killer.

He clipped the badge onto his shoulder holster where once there'd been a different badge, for Houston PD. There he'd been a detective. But Landon had given that up when Emmett was murdered, so he could come home and find the killer.

Too bad it didn't look as if he would find him or her here.

"I'll see you back at the sheriff's office," Landon said, heading toward his truck. It was only about a fifteen-minute ride back into town, not nearly enough time for him to burn off this restless energy churning inside him.

This is for you, Landon.

The words flashed through his head and twisted his gut into a knot so tight that Landon felt sick. Because that was what the handwritten note had said. The note that had been left on Emmett's body. Someone had killed Emmett because of Landon.

But why?

Landon had thought long and hard on it, and he still couldn't figure it out. Since he'd been a Houston cop for nearly a decade, it was possible this was a revenge killing. He'd certainly riled enough criminals over the years, and this could have been a payback murder meant to strike Landon right in the heart.

And it had.

Somewhere, the answers had to be in his old case files. Or maybe in the sketchy details they'd gotten from witnesses about the hours leading up to Emmett's death. Something was there. He just had to find it.

He took the final turn toward town, and Landon saw something he sure as hell didn't want to see.

Smoke.

It was thick, black and coiling from what was left of a barn at the old Waterson place. The house and outbuildings had been vacant for months now since Mr. Waterson had died, but that smoke meant someone was there.

Landon sped toward the blaze and skidded to a stop about twenty yards away. He made a quick 911 call to alert the fire department, and he drew his gun just in case the person responsible for that blaze was still around. However, it was hard to see much of anything, because of the smoke. It was stinging his eyes and making him cough.

But he did hear something.

A stray cat, maybe. Because there shouldn't be any livestock still inside that barn.

Landon went to the back of the barn, or rather what was left of it, and he saw something that had his heart slamming into overdrive.

Not a cat. A woman.

She had shoulder-length brown hair and was on her side, moaning in pain. But she was only a couple of feet from the fire, and the flames were snapping toward her.

Cursing, Landon rushed to her just as the gust of the autumn wind whipped some of those flames right at him. He had to put up his arm to protect his face, and in the same motion, he grabbed her by the ankle, the first part of her he could reach, and he dragged her away from the fire.

Not a second too soon.

A huge chunk of the barn came down with a loud swoosh and sent a spray of fiery timbers and ashes to the very spot where they'd just been. Some of the embers landed on his shirt, igniting it, and Landon had to slap them out before they became full-fledged flames.

The woman moaned again, but he didn't look back at her. He kept moving, kept dragging her until they were finally away from the fire. Well, the fire itself, anyway. The smoke continued to come right at them, and it sent both Landon and her into coughing fits.

And that was when he heard that catlike sound again.

Landon dropped down on his knees, putting himself between the woman and what was left of the fire. Part of the barn was still standing, but it wouldn't be for much longer. He didn't want them anywhere near it when it finally collapsed.

"Are you okay?" he asked her, rolling her to her back so he could see her face. Except he couldn't see much of her face until he wiped off some of the soot.

Ah, hell.

Tessa.

He felt a punch of relief because she was obviously alive after all. But it was a very brief punch because she could be hurt. Dying, even.

Landon checked her for injuries. He couldn't see any obvious ones, but she was holding something wrapped in a soot-covered blanket. He eased it back and was certain his mouth dropped open.

What the heck?

It was a baby.

A newborn, from the looks of it, and he or she was making that kitten sound.

"Whose child is that?" he asked. "And why are you here?"

Those were just two other questions Landon had to add to the list of things he would ask Tessa. And she would answer. Especially answer why Emmett's body was found in her house and where the heck she'd been for the past four days.

"You have to help me," Tessa whispered, her voice barely audible.

Yeah, he did have to help. Just because he didn't like or trust her, that didn't mean he wouldn't save her. Landon didn't want to move her any farther, though, in case she was injured, so he fired off a text to get an ambulance on the way.

Both the baby and she had no doubt inhaled a lot of smoke, but at least the baby's face didn't have any soot on it, which meant maybe the blanket had protected him or her.

"Did you hear me?" he snapped. "Why were you near the burning barn? And whose baby is that?"

He wanted to ask about that dyed hair, too, but it could wait. Though it was likely a dye job to change her appearance.

Landon couldn't think of a good reason for her to do that. But he could think of a really bad one—she was on the run and didn't want anyone to recognize her. Well, she'd picked a stupid place to hide.

If that was what she'd been doing.

She stared up at him. Blinked several times. "Who are you?" she asked.

Landon gave her a flat look. "Very funny. I'm not in the mood for games. Answer those questions I asked and then tell me about Emmett."

"Emmett?" she repeated. She touched her hand to her head, her fingers sliding through her hair. She looked at the ends of the dark strands as if seeing them for the first time. "What did you do to me?"

Landon huffed. "I saved your life. And the baby's."

At the mention of the word *baby*, Landon got a bad feeling.

He quickly did the math, and it'd been seven months, more or less, since he'd landed in bed with Tessa. And he hadn't laid eyes on her since. Seven months might mean…

"Is that our baby?" he demanded.

As she'd done with her hair, she looked down at the newborn who was squirming in her arms. Tessa didn't gasp, but it was close. Her gaze flew to his, the accusation all over her face.

"I don't know," she said, her breath gusting now.

That wasn't the right answer. In fact, that wasn't an acceptable answer at all.

He didn't hold Tessa in high regard, but she would know who'd fathered her child. If it was indeed Landon, she might also be trying to keep the baby from him. After all, they hadn't parted on good terms, and those *terms* had gotten significantly worse with Emmett's murder.

Damn.

Were Tessa and he parents?

No. They couldn't be. The kid had to be Joel Mercer's and hers, and even though Landon had plenty of other reasons for his stomach to knot, just thinking of Joel's name did it. That night, seven months ago, Tessa had sworn she was through with Joel, but Landon would bet his next two paychecks that she had gone right back to him.

She always did.

In the distance, Landon heard the wail of the sirens from the fire engine. It'd be here soon. The ambulance, too. And then Tessa would be whisked away to the hospital, where she could pull another disappearing act.

"Start talking," Landon demanded, getting right in her face. "Tell me everything, and I mean *everything*."

The baby and the ends of her brown hair weren't the only thing she looked at as though she'd never seen them before. Tessa gave Landon that same look.

"Who are you?" she repeated, her eyes filling with tears. "Whose baby is this?" Tessa stopped, those teary blue eyes widening. "And who am *I*?"

Chapter Two

She couldn't catch her breath. Couldn't slow down her pulse. Nor could she fight back the tears that were stinging her eyes. Her heart seemed to be beating out of her chest, and everything inside her was spiraling out of control.

Where was she?

And who was this man staring at her?

Except it wasn't only a stare. He was glaring, and she could tell from the tone of his voice that he was furious with her.

But why?

With the panic building, she frantically studied his face. Dark brown hair. Gray eyes. He was dressed like a cowboy, in jeans, a white shirt and that hat. But he also had a gun.

God, he had a gun.

Gasping, she scrambled to get away from him. She was in danger. She didn't know why or from what, but she had to run.

She clutched the baby closer to her. The baby

wasn't familiar to her, either, but there was one thought that kept repeating in her head.

Protect her.

She knew instinctively that it was a baby girl, and she was in danger. Maybe from this glaring man. Maybe from someone else, but she couldn't risk staying here to find out. Somehow she managed to get to her feet.

"What the hell do you think you're doing?" the man snarled.

She didn't answer. It felt as if all the muscles in her legs had disappeared, and the world started to spin around, but that didn't stop her. She took off running.

However, she didn't get far.

The man caught her almost immediately, and he dragged them to the ground. Not a slam. It was gentle, and he eased his hands around hers to cradle the baby. While she was thankful he was being so careful, that didn't mean she could trust him.

She heard the sirens getting louder with each passing second. Soon, very soon, there'd be others, and she might not be able to trust them, either.

"I have to go," she said, struggling again to get away from him.

But the man held on. "Tessa, stop it!"

She froze. *Tessa?* Was that really her name? She repeated it several times and knew that it was. Finally, something was clear. Her name was Tessa, and she was somewhere on a farm or ranch. Near a burning building. And this man had saved her.

Maybe.

Or maybe he just wanted her to think that so she wouldn't try to run away from him.

"How do you know me?" she asked.

He gave her that look again. The one that told her the answer was obvious. It wasn't, not to her, anyway. But he must have known plenty about her, because he'd asked if the baby was theirs.

She didn't know if it was.

Mercy, she didn't know.

"You know damn well who I am," he snapped. "I'm Landon Ryland."

That felt familiar, too, and it stirred some different feelings inside her. Both good and bad. But Tessa couldn't latch on to any of the specific memories that went with those feelings. Her head was spinning like an F5 tornado.

"Landon," she repeated. And she caught on to one of those memories. Or maybe it was pieces of that jumble that were coming together the wrong way. "I was in bed with you. You were naked."

That didn't help his glare, and she had no idea if she'd actually seen him without clothes or if her mind was playing tricks on her. If so, it was a pretty clear *trick*.

A fire engine squealed to a stop, the lights and sirens still going, but Tessa ignored them for the time being, and she gave the man a harder look. She saw the badge then. He was a lawman. But that didn't put her at ease, and she wasn't sure why.

"Can I trust you?" she came out and asked.

He grunted, and then he studied her. "Is this an act or what?"

Tessa shook her head. Not a good idea, because it brought on the dizziness again. And the panic. "I don't remember who I am," she admitted, her voice collapsing into a sob.

He mumbled some profanity and stood when one of the firemen hurried toward them. "An ambulance is on the way," the fireman said. "Is she hurt?"

"Maybe. But there's also a baby with her."

That put some concern on the fireman's face. Concern in her, too, and she pulled back the blanket to make sure the baby was okay. Something she should have done minutes ago. But it was just so hard to think, so hard to figure out what to do.

The baby was wearing a pink onesie, and she appeared to be all right. Her mouth was puckered as if she were sucking at a bottle, and she was still squirming a little but not actually fussing. Tessa couldn't see any injuries, thank God, and she seemed to be breathing normally.

"I'll tell the ambulance to hurry," the fireman said, moving away from them.

And he wasn't the only one rushing. The firemen were trying to put out the rest of the blaze, not that there was much to save. There were also other sirens, and she saw the blue lights of a cop car as it approached.

She caught on to Landon's hand when he got up and started toward that car. "Please don't let anyone hurt the baby."

That seemed to insult him. "No one will hurt her. Or you. But you will tell me what I need to know."

Tessa didn't think this had anything to do with that memory of them being in bed, but she had no idea what he expected from her. Whatever it was, he clearly expected a lot.

Landon pulled his hand out of her grip and started toward the man who stepped from the cop car. The second man was tall, built just like Landon.

A brother, perhaps?

The second man and Landon talked for several moments, and she saw the surprise register on the other man's face. He kept that same expression as he made his way to her.

"Tessa," he said. Not exactly a friendly greeting. "I'm Deputy Dade Ryland. Landon's cousin," he added, probably because she didn't say anything or show any signs of recognizing him. "We need to ask you some questions before the ambulance gets here."

Tessa nodded because she didn't know what else to do. The baby and she were at the mercy of these men. Her instincts told her, though, that she should get away, run, the first chance she got.

Maybe that chance would come soon. Before it was too late.

But it wasn't Dade who asked any questions. It was Landon. He put his hands on his hips and stared down at her. "We need to know what happened to Emmett."

"He's dead," she blurted out without even realizing she was going to say it. "And so is his wife, Annie. Annie was killed in a car accident."

Where had that come from?

"That's right," Dade said, exchanging an uneasy glance with Landon. "Emmett and Annie are both dead." As Landon had done earlier, Dade knelt down, checking the baby. Then Tessa. Specifically, he looked into her eyes. "She's been drugged," he added to Landon.

"Yeah," Landon readily agreed.

The relief rushed through her. That was why she couldn't remember. But just as quickly, Tessa took that one step further.

Who had drugged her?

The drug had obviously messed with her head. And maybe had done a whole lot more to the rest of her body.

She had a dozen bad possibilities hit her at once, but first and foremost was that if someone had drugged her, they could have done the same to the baby.

The panic came again, hard and fast. "Did they give the baby something, too?"

"I don't think so," Dade said at the same moment that Landon demanded, "Tell me about the baby."

Tessa latched on to what Dade said about the baby, but she had to be sure that the newborn hadn't been drugged. It was something they'd be able to tell her at the hospital.

It's not safe there.

The words knifed through her head, and she repeated them aloud. And something else, too. "Don't trust anyone."

They weren't her words but something someone else had said to her. Important words. But Tessa didn't know who'd told her that.

Or why.

Obviously, that didn't make Landon happy. He said some more profanity. Added another glare. "She keeps dodging questions about the baby."

That caused Dade to give her another look. This time not to her eyes but rather her stomach. Not that he could see much of it, because she was holding the baby, but he was no doubt trying to see if she had recently given birth.

"Did you set this fire?" Dade asked her, easing the baby's legs away from Tessa's belly.

Tessa flinched, and Dade must have thought he'd hurt her, because he backed off. But that wasn't the reason she'd reacted that way. She'd winced not from pain but from his question.

"Someone set the fire?" she asked.

Landon didn't roll his eyes, but it was close. "Take a whiff of the air."

She did and got a quick reminder of the smoke. The breeze was blowing it away from them now, but Tessa could still smell it. And she could also smell something else.

Gasoline.

"Someone, maybe you," Landon continued, "used an accelerant. Based on how the fire spread, I'm guessing it was poured near the front of the barn and was ignited there."

And the person had done that while the baby and she were still inside.

Oh, mercy. That was a memory that came at her full force with not just the smells but the sensation on her skin. The hot flames licking at her. Her, running. Trying to get away from…someone.

She also remembered the fear.

"Someone tried to kill me," she said.

Dade didn't argue with that, but it was obvious she hadn't convinced Landon. Well, she didn't need to convince him. There weren't many things Tessa was certain of, but she was positive that she'd just come close to being murdered. Or maybe the person who'd set that fire had been trying to flush her out.

But why would she have been hiding in that barn?

Tessa didn't get to say more about that, and maybe she wouldn't have anyway, because the ambulance came driving toward them. The moment the vehicle stopped, two paramedics scrambled out, carrying a stretcher, and they headed straight for her and the baby.

She studied their faces as they approached, trying to see if she knew them. She didn't, but then, no one looked familiar. Well, except for Landon, and she didn't have enough information to know if she could trust him.

Don't trust anyone.

But if she hadn't trusted Landon, why had she landed in bed with him?

After cutting his way past Dade and Landon, one of the medics checked her. The other, the baby. And they asked questions. A flurry of them that she couldn't answer. How old was the baby? Any medical history of allergies? Were either of them taking medications?

"She claims she doesn't remember anything," Landon snarled. "Well, almost nothing. She knows Emmett's dead."

Yes. She did know that. But that was it. Heck, she wasn't even sure who Emmett was, but even through her hazy mind, it was obvious that these two lawmen believed she knew a whole lot more than she was saying.

Or maybe they believed she was the reason he was dead.

While Tessa kept a firm hold on the baby, the paramedics lifted them both onto the stretcher. "Will you be riding in the ambulance with them?" one of them asked Landon.

Landon stared at her, nodded. "Please tell me once these drugs wear off that she'll be able to remember everything."

"You know I can't guarantee that. She's been injured, too. Looks like someone hit her on the head."

Landon glanced back at the barn. "She could have gotten it there. When I got here, she was on the ground moaning. Maybe something fell on her."

The paramedic made a sound of disagreement. "It didn't happen today. More like a couple of days ago."

"Around the time when Emmett was killed,"

Landon said under his breath, and he looked ready to launch into another round of questions that Tessa knew she couldn't—and maybe *shouldn't*—answer.

However, one of the firemen hurried toward them, calling out for Landon before he reached him. "You need to see this," the fireman insisted.

Landon cursed and started to walk away, but then he stopped and stabbed his finger at her. "Don't you dare go anywhere. I'm riding in the ambulance with you to make sure you get there."

It sounded like some kind of threat. Felt like one, too.

The paramedics lifted the stretcher, moving the baby and her toward the ambulance, but they were also carrying her in the same direction Landon was headed. Tessa watched as the fireman led him to the front of what was left of the barn.

Whatever the fireman wanted Landon to see, it was on the ground, because both men stooped, their attention on a large gray boulder. Dade did the same when he joined them.

She saw Landon's shoulder's snap back, and it seemed as if he was cursing again. He pulled his phone from his pocket and took a picture, and after saying something to Dade, he came toward her. Not hurrying exactly, but with that fierce expression, he looked like an Old West cowboy who was about to draw in a gunfight.

"What do you know about this?" Landon demanded. "Did you write it?" He held up his phone screen for her to see.

With everything around her swimming in and out of focus, it took Tessa a few seconds to make out the words. When she did, she felt as if a Mack truck had just slammed into her.

Oh. God.

Chapter Three

While he waited on hold for Dade to come back on
the line, Landon glanced around the thin blue curtain to check on Tessa again. Something he'd been
doing since they arrived at the Silver Creek Hospital.
She was still sitting on the examining table, feeding
the baby a bottle of formula that the hospital staff
had given her.

Tessa was also still eyeing Landon as if he were
the enemy.

That probably had plenty to do with the message
that'd been scrawled on the boulder back at the barn.
This is for you, Landon.

The same words as in the message that'd been left
on Emmett's body. Except this time, there was a little
more. *Tessa's dead now because of you.*

Reading that obviously hadn't helped lessen the
fear he'd seen in Tessa's eyes. Hadn't helped this knot
in Landon's stomach, either. He had to find out what
was going on, and that started with Tessa.

She'd insisted on the baby staying with her, so
they had both been placed in the same room, where

the doctor was checking them now. Maybe the doc would be able to give her something to counteract whatever drug Tessa had been given.

Or taken.

But Landon had to shake his head at that thought. Tessa wasn't a drug user, so someone had likely given it to her. He needed to know why.

This is for you, Landon.

Someone clearly had it out for him. And that someone had murdered Emmett and had maybe now tried to do the same thing to Tessa and that innocent baby.

The baby had to be cleared up for him, too. If she was his child... Well, Landon didn't want to go there just yet. He already had enough to juggle without having to deal with that. The only thing that mattered now was that the baby got whatever medical attention she needed, and Landon could go from there.

"There were no prints on the boulder," Dade said when he finally came back on the line.

Landon groaned, but he really hadn't expected they would get that lucky. The person who'd set all of this up wouldn't have been stupid enough to leave prints behind. But he or she had left a witness.

One whose memory was a mess.

"The crime scene folks will do a more thorough check, of course," Dade went on. "Something might turn up. Anything from Tessa yet?"

"Nothing. The nurse drew her and the baby's blood when they got here. Once we have the results of the tox screen, we'll know what drug she was given. And if that's what is affecting her memory."

Of course, there was still that lump on her head.

The doctor had examined it, too, right after checking the baby, but like the paramedic, the doc said it was an injury that Tessa had gotten several days ago. In the doctor's opinion, it was the result of blunt-force trauma.

Landon figured the timing wasn't a coincidence.

"I don't think she's faking this memory loss," Landon added to Dade.

Tessa must have heard that, because her gaze slashed to his. Of course, her attention hadn't stayed too far away from him since this whole ordeal started. And after seeing that message on the rock, he knew why.

"All of this is definitely connected to me," Landon said to Dade. "The second message proves it."

Or at least, that was what someone wanted him to believe—that both Emmett's murder and this attack were because of something Landon had done.

"Did you find anything else in the old arrest records you've been going through?" Dade asked.

Landon had found plenty. Too much, in fact. It was hard to narrow down a pool of suspects when Landon could name several dozen criminals that he'd had run-ins with over the years. But there was one that kept turning up like a bad penny.

"Quincy Nagel," Landon answered. The name wouldn't surprise his cousin, because Landon had discussed Quincy with Grayson, Dade and the other deputies in Silver Creek.

Landon had put Quincy behind bars four years ago for breaking and entering. Quincy had sworn to get even, and he was out on probation now. That made him a prime suspect. Except for one thing.

Quincy was in a wheelchair.

The man had been paralyzed from the waist down in a prison fight. It would have taken some strength to overpower Emmett and to club Tessa on the head. Strength or a hired thug. But while Quincy had plenty of money from his trust fund to hire a thug, there was no money trail to indicate Quincy had done that.

"I'll keep looking," Landon said to Dade. Though the looking would have to wait for now, because the doctor stepped away from Tessa, and that was Landon's cue to go in the room.

Landon knew the doctor. Doug Michelson. He'd been a fixture in Silver Creek for years, and while Landon had moved away when he was a kid, he still remembered the doc giving him checkups and tending to him on the various emergency room trips that he'd had to make.

"The baby's fine," Dr. Michelson said right off. "But I want to get a pediatrician in here to verify that. I'm guessing she's less than a week old since she still has her umbilical cord."

Since Landon didn't have a clue what to say about that, he just nodded.

"Is she yours?" Dr. Michelson asked.

Landon didn't know what to say about that, either, so he lifted his shoulder. "I'm hoping Tessa can tell me."

The doctor scratched his head. "Probably not at the moment but maybe soon she can do that. I can use the baby's blood test to run her DNA if you give me the go-ahead."

"You've definitely got the go-ahead for that. And put a rush on it just in case Tessa's memory doesn't come back."

"Will do. I did manage to get Tessa to let a nurse hold the baby so I could get an X-ray of her neck," the doctor continued, but he stopped, obviously noticing the renewed surprise on Landon's face.

"What's wrong with Tessa's neck?" Landon asked.

"She's got a small lesion." The doctor pointed to the area where his neck and shoulders met. "It's too big for it to be an injection site for the drugs she was given. Besides, I found the needle mark for that. Or rather the needle *marks*. There are two of them on her arm. One is at least a couple of days old, and there was bruising involved."

"Bruising that probably happened around the same time she was hit on the head?" Landon asked.

"Yes. The other is more recent. I'd say an injection given to her within the last couple of hours."

So she'd been drugged twice. "Then what's with the lesion?"

The doctor shrugged. "I might know once I've had a chance to look at the X-ray. For now, though, I need to get an OB in here to examine Tessa."

Landon heard something in the doc's voice. Concern maybe? "You think something's wrong?"

"She doesn't trust me, so I'm thinking she might not trust an OB to do an exam, either. But an exam is a must since we have to rule out problems other than just the head injury." The doctor patted Landon's arm. "Talk to her. Convince her we're the good guys."

He'd have an easier time convincing Tessa that the sun was green. Still, he'd try. Plus, the doctor didn't give him much of a choice. He headed out, no doubt to round up the OB and pediatrician, leaving Landon alone with Tessa and the baby.

"Tell me what's going on," Tessa demanded.

Since that was what Landon wanted to ask her, they were at an impasse. One that he hoped they could work through fast. While he was hoping, he needed those drugs to wear off—now.

"Tell me," she snapped when he didn't jump to answer.

He didn't jump because Landon wasn't sure where to start. The beginning seemed like a lifetime ago.

"Stop me at any point if this is old news," he began. "A year ago, you moved to Silver Creek to open a private investigations office. We met shortly afterward, had a few dates, and I ran into you again at the Outlaw Bar when I was in town visiting my cousins."

He paused, waiting for her to process that. "Is that when you were naked in bed with me?" she asked, setting the baby bottle down beside her.

Of course she would remember *that*. But then, if the baby was his, she probably had it etched in her memory. Landon had it etched in his for a different reason. Because of the white-hot attraction that'd been between them.

But that wasn't something he needed to remember now. Or ever.

"Yes. The following morning, you told me you couldn't get involved with me," Landon continued. "And then your scummy boyfriend showed up. Joel Mercer. Remember him?"

She repeated the name, shook her head. "If I had a boyfriend, why did I sleep with you?"

Landon had asked himself that many, many times. "You said he was an ex, but he sure didn't act like it." He stopped, huffed. "Look, are you sure you don't remember simply because you'd rather not be talking about this with me?"

"I'm not faking or avoiding this conversation. Now, tell me about Joel. Why did you say he's scummy?"

"Because he is. He's a cattle broker—at least, that's what he calls himself, but it's really a front for assorted felonies, including gunrunning and money laundering. That's why I was surprised when he showed up and said you two were together."

Judging from her expression, Tessa was surprised, too. But it wasn't the same kind of surprise that'd been on her face that morning seven months ago. Landon had seen the shock, and then she'd changed.

Or something. She'd become all lovey-dovey with Joel and told Landon to leave.

But Landon hadn't forgotten the look that'd gone through her eyes.

After he'd walked, or rather stormed, out, he'd gone back to Houston and hadn't seen her since. And apparently neither had any of his cousins. Tessa had closed her PI office, and while she'd kept her house in Silver Creek, she rarely visited it.

That was maybe why no one had known she was pregnant.

Because if his cousins had known, they would have told Landon. Plenty of people, including a couple of his cousins, had seen him leave the Outlaw Bar with Tessa that night.

"What does Joel have to do with Emmett?" she asked.

Everything inside him went still. Until now he hadn't considered they could be connected.

But were they?

Landon decided to try something to jog her memory. "Four nights ago, someone murdered Emmett in your house." Man, it was still hard to say that aloud. Just as hard to think about his cousin dying that way. "Your cleaning lady found his body. He'd been shot three times, and there was a note left on his chest."

"'This is for you, Landon,'" she whispered.

"How the hell did you know that?" He hadn't intended to raise his voice, and the baby reacted. She started to whimper.

"I'm not sure. But I saw your reaction when Dade

showed you what was on the boulder. I guessed it must have been something to do with Emmett since the majority of your questions had been about him." She rocked the baby, kissed her forehead. "And her."

Yeah. And he would have more questions about *her* when he was finished with this.

Landon took out his phone, and even though he knew the picture was gruesome, he searched through his pictures and found the one he'd taken at the crime scene.

Emmett's body in a pool of blood.

There'd been blood on the note, too.

"Does this look familiar?" Landon asked, putting the phone practically in her face.

She gasped, turned her head and closed her eyes for a moment. "No." And she repeated it in a hoarse sob.

Landon didn't have a heart of ice. Not completely, anyway, and whether he wanted to or not, he was affected by that look on her face. Affected, but not to the point where he was stopping with the questions.

"Why was Emmett there at your house, and how did you know he was dead?" he pressed.

She shook her head. "I honestly don't know." Tessa paused, swallowed hard. "There's something about that photo that seems familiar, but I don't know what."

Good. Because if it was familiar, then it meant she was possibly there and might have seen who had done this.

Landon went to the next picture. A mug shot this time of Quincy Nagel. "Recognize him?"

Tessa moved closer for a long look and gave him another head shake. "Who is he?"

"A person of interest." Too bad Landon hadn't been able to find him yet. "A thug I arrested who might have wanted to pay me back by killing my cousin."

Tessa kept her attention on the baby, but because Landon was watching her so closely, he saw the small change in her. Her mouth tensed. A muscle flexed in her cheek. He hoped that was because she was concerned for the baby rather than because she was withholding something about Quincy. The little girl went beyond the whimpering stage and started to cry.

"So I slept with you, got pregnant." Tessa stood and rocked the baby. "Or maybe you believe she's Joel's daughter? You're not sure, but you'll demand a test so you can be certain."

He nodded. Though he would be surprised if she was Joel's. Yes, Tessa had been more than just friendly with Joel, but Landon didn't think she was the sort to go from one man straight to another. But he'd been wrong about stuff like that before. He didn't think so this time, though.

"Or maybe she's not my baby at all," she added. Tessa shuddered, dodged his gaze.

Landon lifted her chin, forcing eye contact. "Are you remembering something?"

"No."

Her answer came much too fast, and Landon

would have jumped right on that if his phone hadn't buzzed. It was Grayson, which meant it could have something to do with the investigation. Since the baby was still crying, Landon stepped just into the hall so he could hear what the sheriff had to say.

"We found something," Grayson said the moment Landon answered. "A car on a ranch trail not far from the barn. The plates are fake, the VIN's been removed, but it has some baby things in it. A diaper bag and some clothes."

Tessa's car.

Or one that she'd "borrowed."

"We'll process it, of course," Grayson went on, "but something really stuck out. The GPS was programmed to go to your house in Houston."

Landon wanted to say that wasn't right, that there'd been no reason for her to see him, but if the baby was indeed his, maybe Tessa had been on the way to tell him. Of course, that didn't explain the other things: the dyed hair, the hit on her head, fake tags, no vehicle identification number on the car. Those were all signs of someone trying to hide.

Landon stepped out of the doorway when he saw Dr. Michelson approaching. There were two other doctors with him. The pediatrician and the OB, no doubt, and maybe one of them could talk Tessa into having the examination.

"What about the area leading from the car to the barn?" Landon asked Grayson. "Were there any signs of a struggle?"

"None, but something might turn up. In the meantime, ask Tessa why she was going to see you. Hearing about the GPS might trigger her memory."

He ended the call, intending to do just that, but Dr. Michelson pulled back the blue curtain and looked at him. "Where's Tessa and the baby?"

Landon practically pushed the doctor aside and looked into the room. No Tessa. No baby. But the door leading off the back of the examining room was open.

Damn.

"Close off all the exits," Landon told the doctor, and he took off after her.

He cursed Tessa, and himself, for this. He should have known she would run, and when he caught up with her, she'd better be able to explain why she'd done this.

Landon barreled through the adjoining room. Another exam room, crammed with equipment that he had to maneuver around. He also checked the corners in case she had ducked behind something with plans to sneak out after he'd zipped right past her.

But she wasn't there, either.

There was a hall just off the examining room, and Landon headed there, his gaze slashing from one end of it to the other. He didn't see her.

But he heard something.

The baby.

She was still crying, and even though the sound was muffled, it was enough for Landon to pinpoint their location. Tessa was headed for the back exit. Landon doubted the doctor had managed to get the doors locked yet, so he hurried, running as fast as he could.

And then he saw her.

Tessa saw him, too.

She didn't stop. With the baby gripped in her arms, she threw open the glass door and was within a heartbeat of reaching the parking lot. She might have made it, too, but Landon took hold of her arms and pulled her back inside.

As he'd done by the barn, he was as gentle with her as he could be, but he wasn't feeling very much of that gentleness inside.

Tessa was breathing through her mouth. Her eyes were wide. And she groaned. "I remember," she said.

He jerked back his head. That was the last thing Landon had expected her to say, but he'd take it. "Yeah, and you're going to tell me everything you remember, and you're going to do it right now."

But she didn't. Tessa just stood there, her attention volleying between him and the parking lot.

"Please, just let me go." Her eyes filled with tears. "It's not safe for you to be with me."

"What the hell does that mean?" Landon snapped.

She closed her eyes, the tears spilling down her cheeks. "I'm not who you think I am. And if you stay here with me, they'll kill you."

Chapter Four

Tessa tried to move away from Landon again, but he held on to her.

"Explain that," he demanded.

She didn't have to ask exactly what he wanted her to tell him. It was about the bombshell she'd just delivered.

If you stay here with me, they'll kill you.

There were plenty of things still unclear in Tessa's head, but that wasn't one of them.

She glanced behind her at the parking lot on the other side of the glass door. "It's not safe for us to be here. Please, let's go somewhere else."

Landon stared at her, obviously debating that, and he finally maneuvered her to the side. Not ideal, but it was better than being in front of the glass, where she could be seen, and at least this way she had a view of the hall in case someone came at her from that direction.

"Now that the drugs are wearing off, I'm remembering some things about Emmett's murder," Tessa admitted.

His eyes narrowed. "Keep talking."

"I didn't see the killer's face." Though Tessa tried to picture him, the bits and pieces of her memory didn't cooperate. "I came into my house, and this man wearing a ski mask attacked me. Emmett was there, and they fought."

Landon stayed quiet for a long time, clearly trying to process that. "Why was Emmett there?"

She had to shake her head. "I don't know. I don't know why the other man was there, either. Maybe he was a burglar?"

That didn't sound right at all, though. No. He wasn't a burglar, but clearly there were still some blanks in her memory. And because he was wearing a ski mask, she didn't have even fragmented memories of seeing his face.

Tessa looked down at the baby. Did that man have something to do with the newborn?

"A *burglar*," Landon repeated, "wouldn't have left a note like that on Emmett's body. His killer was connected to me and obviously to you since the murder happened in your house." He tipped his head to the baby. "And where was she the whole time this attack on you was going on?"

"In my arms." Tessa was certain of that. "She was also in my arms when I ran from the man. No, wait." More images came. Then the memory of the pain exploding in her head. "He hit me with his gun first." That explained the bump on her head. "Emmett tried to stop him, and that's when I think the man shot him."

Landon dropped back a step, no doubt taking a moment to absorb that. Those details were still fuzzy, and Tessa was actually thankful for it. She wasn't sure that right now she could handle remembering a man being murdered. Especially so soon after nearly dying in that barn fire.

"You were close to Emmett?" she asked but then waved off the question. Of course he was. And apparently she had been, too.

After all, Emmett had been at her house.

"I think his killer might have been a cop," Tessa added.

Landon huffed. "First a burglar, now a cop?"

She didn't blame him for being skeptical, but her mind was all over the place, and it was so hard to think, especially with that warning that kept going through her head.

That it wasn't safe here. That she couldn't trust anyone.

That she was going to get Landon killed.

"The killer held his gun like a cop," she explained. "And he had one of those ear communicators like cops use."

"Criminals use them, too," Landon was just as quick to point out.

True enough. "But he said something about a perp to whoever he was talking to on the communicator. That's a word that cops use." Tessa paused. "And when I saw your badge, I got scared. Because I thought maybe... Well, it doesn't matter what I thought."

"You thought I had killed Emmett," he finished for her. Landon added a sharp glare to that. "I didn't, and I need you to remember a whole lot more than you just told me."

So did she, but before Tessa could even consider how to make that happen, she saw some movement in the hall. Landon saw it, too, because he moved in front of her. From over his shoulder, Tessa saw Dr. Michelson and a security guard. But there was another man with him. Tall and lanky with blond hair. Wearing a suit. It took her a moment to get a good look at his face.

Her heart jumped to her throat.

"Joel," she said. Even with the dizziness, she recognized him.

Landon looked back at her, a new round of displeasure in his expression. "So you remember him now?"

She did. And unlike the other memories, these were a lot clearer.

Oh, God.

This could be bad.

Joel kept his attention on her, obviously studying her dyed hair, but she soon saw the recognition in his eyes, and he picked up the pace as he made his way toward her.

"Tessa?" Joel called out. "Are you all right?"

Landon didn't budge. He stayed in front of her. "Someone tried to kill her. What do you know about that?"

Until Landon barked out that question, Joel hadn't

seemed to notice him. But he noticed him now. "What are *you* doing here?" Joel snapped.

Landon tapped his badge. "What I'm doing is asking you a question that you *will* answer right now."

Despite the fact that Landon's tone was as lethal as his expression, Joel made a sound of amusement when he glanced at the badge. "What happened? Did you lose your job as a Houston cop and have to come begging your cousin for work?"

That jogged her memory, too. Yes, Landon had been a detective with the Houston PD, but Tessa doubted he'd lost his job. He had likely come back to Silver Creek to solve Emmett's murder. Good thing, too, or else there might not have been anyone to save her from that barn fire.

But he couldn't help her get out of this.

"How did you know I was at the hospital?" Tessa asked Joel.

Obviously, that wasn't what he wanted to hear from her. He probably expected a much warmer greeting, because he stepped around Landon and reached out as if to hug her.

Landon, however, blocked his path. "How did you know she was here?" he pressed.

Joel looked at her. Then at Landon. And it must have finally sunk in that this was not a good time for a social visit. If that was indeed what it was.

"What happened to you?" Joel asked her.

"I'm not sure." That was only a partial lie. "Someone drugged me and then tried to kill me."

Joel nodded. "In the barn fire. My assistant got a

call from a friend who works at the fire department. He told her that you'd been brought here to the Silver Creek Hospital. I came right away."

"Why?" Landon demanded.

Joel huffed as if the answer were obvious, but he snapped back toward Tessa when the baby made a whimpering sound. He peered around Landon, and Tessa watched Joel's face carefully so she could try to gauge his reaction.

He was shocked.

She hadn't thought for a second that the baby was his, because Tessa was certain she'd never slept with Joel. She definitely didn't have any memories of him being naked in her bed. But she'd considered that he might have known if she'd had a child.

If she had, that is.

Joel stepped back, the shock fading, and in his eyes, she saw something else. The raw anger, some directed at her. Most of it, though, was directed at Landon.

"You two had a baby," Joel snapped. "That's why I haven't heard from you in months."

Months? Had it been that long? Mercy, she needed to remember.

"I didn't think things were serious with you two," Joel added. "You said it was just a one-time fling with him."

She figured Joel had purposely used the word *fling* to make it seem as if what'd happened between Landon and her had been trivial. Of course, that was exactly what she'd led Joel, and even Landon, to believe.

Tessa needed to settle some things with Joel, but she couldn't do that now. Not with the baby here. And not until she was certain that this jumble of memories was right.

"I want the name of the person from the fire department who contacted your assistant and told her about Tessa," Landon continued.

It took Joel a few moments to pull his stare from her and look at Landon. "I'll have to get that for you. My assistant didn't mention a name, and I didn't think to ask."

Well, it was a name that Tessa needed so she'd know if Joel had someone in the Silver Creek Fire Department who was on the take.

"I'll want that information within the next half hour," Landon added. "And now you'll have to leave because Tessa and the baby have to be examined by the doctors."

Joel turned to her as if he expected her to ask him to stay. And she might have if Tessa had had the energy to keep up the facade so she could try to get what info she could from Joel. She didn't. It was time to regroup and tell Landon what she'd remembered, but she couldn't do that in front of Joel.

"Landon's right. The baby and I need to be examined," Tessa stated to Joel. "Please just go."

She could see the debate Joel was having with himself, but Tessa also saw the moment he gave in to her request. "Call me when you're done here,"

Joel said. "We have to talk." And he walked away as if there were no question that she would indeed do just that.

Tessa and Landon stood there watching him, until Joel disappeared around the hall corner.

"I'll need a minute with Tessa," Landon told the doctor and security guard.

The doctor hesitated, maybe because Landon's jaw was clenched and he looked ready to yell at Tessa. But Tessa gave the doctor a nod to let him know it was okay for him to leave. As Landon and she had done with Joel, they waited until both men were out of sight.

Since she knew that Landon was about to launch into an interrogation, Tessa went ahead and got started. "I don't think the baby is ours," she said. "And I'm certain she's not Joel's."

"How would you know that?"

She got another image of Landon naked. Good grief, why was that so clear? It was a distraction she didn't need. Especially since the man himself was right in front of her, reminding her of the reason they'd landed in bed in the first place.

"I just know," she answered. An answer that clearly didn't please him.

"Then whose baby is that?" Landon snapped.

Even though Landon wasn't going to like this, she had to shake her head. "Memories are still fuzzy there, but I don't have any recollection of being pregnant. I think I would have remembered morning sickness, the delivery...something."

"And you don't?"

"Nothing." She wasn't certain if he looked relieved, disappointed or skeptical. But she wasn't lying.

"The doctor will be able to tell once he examines you," Landon reminded her.

She nodded. "I do have plenty of memories about Joel, though." Tessa had to lean against the wall when a new wave of dizziness hit her. "And some memories about me, too. I'm not a real PI."

Landon stared at her as if she were lying. "But you have a PI's license. A real one. I checked."

Of course he had. Landon probably wouldn't have asked her out unless he'd run a basic background check on her. And he definitely wouldn't have slept with her.

Then she rethought that.

The sex hadn't been planned, and it'd happened in the heat of the moment. Literally.

"Yes, I have a license." Best just to toss this out there and then deal with the aftermath. And there would be aftermath. "But I had it only because of Joel. He said he wanted me to get it so I could help him vet some of his business associates. It's easier for a PI to do that because I had access to certain databases."

She got the exact reaction she expected. Landon's eyes narrowed. Tessa wasn't sure of all of Joel's activities, but there were enough of them for her to know the kind of man she was dealing with. Landon had called him scummy, but he was much worse than that.

Because Joel was a dangerous man.

With that reminder, she looked around them again. Tessa could still see the parking lot and the hall, and Landon made an uneasy glance around, too.

"You'll want to keep going with that explanation," Landon insisted. "But remember, you're talking to a cop."

The threat was real. He could arrest her, but it was a risk she had to take right now. She needed Landon on her side so he could help her protect this baby. Maybe from Joel.

Maybe from someone else.

Mercy, it was so hard to think.

Tessa had to clear her throat before she could continue. "I think Joel might have murdered someone."

His eyes were already dark, but that darkened them even more. "Who? Emmett?"

But she didn't get a chance to answer.

Landon stepped in front of her, drawing his weapon. That was when she saw the man in the hall.

He was coming straight toward them.

And he had a gun.

Chapter Five

Landon had a split-second debate with himself about just shooting at the armed man who was coming right at them.

But he couldn't.

It would be a huge risk to start shooting in the hospital around innocent bystanders.

A risk for Tessa and the baby, too.

The man obviously didn't have a problem doing just that. He lifted his gun and took aim. Landon hooked his arm around Tessa and yanked her out of the line of fire.

Barely in time.

The bullet smacked into the concrete block wall where they'd just been standing. The noise was deafening, and the baby immediately started to cry.

Landon pulled Tessa and the baby to the side so that he could use the wall for protection, but it wouldn't protect them for long, because the idiot fired another shot and sent more of those bits of concrete scattering.

"Tessa?" the man called out. "If you want the bullets to stop, then hand the kid to the cowboy cop and come with me."

Because Landon still had hold of her, he felt her muscles turn to iron, and she held the baby even closer to her body.

"Oh, God," she whispered.

Landon mumbled something significantly worse. This was not what he wanted to happen.

Of course, Landon had known there could be another attack since someone had tried to kill Tessa in that barn fire, but he hadn't thought a second attempt would happen in the hospital with so many witnesses around. Plus, the guy wasn't even wearing a mask. That meant he either knew no one would recognize him or didn't care if they did. But whoever he was, one thing was crystal clear.

This thug wanted Tessa.

Later, Landon would want to know why, but he figured this had something to do with one of the last things she'd said to him before the guy started shooting.

I think Joel might have murdered someone.

Landon didn't doubt it for a second. Nor did he doubt this armed thug was connected to Joel. But why exactly did Joel want her? Had she learned something incriminating while she was working for him vetting his "cattle broker" associates?

"Tessa?" the man called out. "You've got ten seconds."

"He knows you," Landon whispered to her. "You recognize his voice?

"No," she answered without hesitating.

"Think about it," the guy added. "Every bullet I fire puts that kid in danger even more. Danger that you can stop by coming with me."

"He's right," Tessa said on a rise of breath.

She moved as if preparing herself to surrender, but Landon wasn't going to let that happen.

"Stay back," he warned her.

Landon leaned out, trying to time it so that he wouldn't get shot, and glanced into the hall. The guy was no longer out in the open. He'd taken cover in a doorway.

Hell.

Hopefully, there wasn't anyone inside the room where this man was hiding or he would no doubt shoot them.

On the second glance, Landon took aim and fired at the moron. The guy ducked back into the room, and Landon's bullets slammed into the door.

He couldn't stand there and trade shots with this guy, because sooner or later, the gunman might get lucky. Certainly by now someone had called the sheriff, and that meant Grayson would be here soon. Although it might not be soon enough.

"Let's go," Landon told her.

He leaned around the corner and fired another shot at the man, and Landon hoped it would pin him in place long enough to put some distance between those bullets and Tessa.

Staying in front of her while trying to keep watch all around them, Landon maneuvered her down the back hall toward the other end, where there was another line of patients' rooms. He prayed that all the patients and staff had heard the shots and were hunkering down somewhere.

The baby was still crying, and even though Tessa was trying to comfort it, her attempts weren't working. Too bad. Because the sounds of the baby's cries were like a homing beacon for that shooter.

Landon had no choice but to pause when he reached the junction of the halls, and he glanced around to see if there was a second gunman waiting to ambush them.

Empty.

Thank God.

But his short pause allowed the shooter to catch up with them. The guy leaned around the corner where Landon had just been, and he fired at them.

Since it was possible for the gunman to double back and come at them from the other end of the hall, Landon needed better protection. Again, it was a risk because he didn't know what he was going to find, but he opened the first door he reached.

Not empty.

And the young twentysomething woman inside gave him a jolt until he noticed that she wore a hospital gown and was hanging on to an IV pole. She was a patient.

He hoped.

"Go in the bathroom," he ordered the woman. "Close the door and don't come out."

She gasped and gave a shaky nod but followed his

instructions. Landon would have liked to have sent Tessa and the baby in there with her, but he couldn't risk it. Anyone bold enough to send this gunman could have also planted backups in the rooms.

"Keep an eye on the woman," Landon whispered to Tessa.

Tessa's eyes widened, probably because she realized this could be a trap. Of course, that was only one of their problems. The baby was still crying, the sound echoing through the empty hall.

Landon heard the footsteps to his right. The gunman, no doubt. And he readied himself to shoot when the man rounded the corner. But the footsteps stopped just short of the hall junction.

He glanced back at Tessa to make sure she was staying down. She was, and she was volleying glances between him and the bathroom door. In those glimpses that Landon got of her face, though, he could see the stark fear in her eyes. He would have liked to assure her that they'd get out of this alive, but Landon had no idea how this would play out.

"Tessa?" the guy called out. "Time's up."

Landon braced himself for more shots. And they came, all right. The guy pivoted around the corner, and he started shooting right at Tessa and him. Landon had no choice but to push her deeper into the room.

"Deputy Ryland?" someone called out. It was the security guard, and judging from the sound of his voice, he was on the opposite end of the hall from the shooter. "The other deputies are in the building. They're on the way now to help you."

Good. Well, maybe. It could be a bluff since it'd been less than ten minutes since the shooting had started, and that would be a very fast response time for backup. Still, even if it was a bluff, it worked.

Because the shots stopped, and Landon heard the guy take off running.

His first instincts were to go after the guy, to stop him from getting away, but Landon had no way of knowing if the security guard was on the take. Hell, this could be a ruse to lure them out of the room so that Tessa could be kidnapped or killed.

Landon waited, cursing while he listened to the thug get away, but it wasn't long before he heard another voice. One that he trusted completely.

Grayson.

"Landon?" his cousin called out. "Don't shoot. I'm coming toward you."

It seemed to take an eternity for Grayson to make it to them, and when he reached the door, Landon could see the concern on his face. Concern that was no doubt mirrored in Landon's own expression.

"Come on," Grayson said, motioning for them to follow him. "I need to get the three of you out of here right now."

TESSA'S HEART WAS beating so hard that she thought her ribs might crack. Her entire body was shaking, especially her legs, and if Landon hadn't hooked his arm around her for support, she would have almost certainly fallen.

She hated feeling like his. Helpless and weak. But at the moment she had no choice but to rely on Landon and Grayson to get the baby and her away from that shooter.

The sheriff led them up the hall, in the opposite direction of where the gunman had fired those last shots. Since that back hall also led to the parking lot, Tessa suspected he was getting away.

That didn't help slow down her heartbeat.

Because if he escaped, he could return for a second attempt. But an attempt at what? He obviously had wanted her to go with him. Or maybe that was what he had wanted her to believe. If she'd surrendered, he could have just gunned her down, done the same to Landon. Heaven knew then what would have happened to the baby.

"This way," Grayson said, and he didn't head toward the front but rather to a side exit.

The moment they reached it, Tessa spotted the cruiser parked there, only inches from the exit and apparently waiting for him. When Grayson opened the door, she saw Dade behind the wheel.

Even though she now believed she could trust the Ryland lawmen, seeing him and Grayson still gave her a jolt. If she'd been right about Emmett's killer being a cop, then it was possible the killer worked at the Silver Creek sheriff's office.

Landon hurried her onto the backseat, following

right behind her, and the moment he shut the door, Dade took off.

"Are you all okay?" Dade asked, making brief eye contact in the rearview mirror.

Landon nodded but then checked her face. Tessa did the same to the baby. The newborn was still making fussing sounds, but she wasn't hurt. Thank God. That was a miracle, what with all those bullets flying.

When she finished examining the baby, Tessa realized Landon was still looking at her. Or rather he was staring at her. No doubt waiting for answers.

Answers that she didn't have.

Someone had attacked her twice in the same day. Heck, maybe even more than that since her memories were still hazy.

"Maybe he's one of Joel's hired thugs?" Landon asked.

She had to shake her head again. Then Tessa had to stop because a new wave of dizziness came over her. It was so hard to think with her head spinning. "I only got a glimpse of him before you pulled me back, but he didn't look familiar. I don't know why he came after me like that. Do you?"

"No," Landon snapped. "But I want you to guess why he attacked us. And the guessing should start with you telling me everything you know about Joel. The baby, too."

His tone wasn't as sharp as it'd been before, and his glare had softened some. Maybe he was starting to believe that this wasn't her fault.

Well, not totally her fault, anyway.

Tessa tried to concentrate and latch on to whatever information she could remember. It was strange, but the memories from years ago were a lot clearer than the recent ones. In fact, some of the recent ones were just a tangle of images and sounds.

"Tell me about Joel," Landon pressed, probably because she was still trying to figure out what to say.

"Joel," she repeated. And Tessa went with what she did remember. "I started working for him two years ago as a bookkeeper. I didn't know what he was," she added. "I was an out-of-work accountant, and he offered me a job. Later, he wanted me to be a PI so I could run background checks for him."

"But you soon found out what he was," Landon finished for her.

Another nod. "But I didn't know how deep his operation went, and he was hiding assets and activities under layers of corporate paperwork." Tessa had to pause again, brush away the mental cobwebs. These next memories were spotty compared to the ones of her starting to work for Joel.

"Back at the hospital, you said you thought Joel had killed someone," Landon reminded her. "Who? Emmett?"

Tessa closed her eyes a moment, trying to make the thoughts come. Finally, she remembered a piece of a memory. Or maybe it was just a dream. It was so hard to work all of this out.

"No. Not Emmett. I think the murder might have had something to do with the baby's mother," she said. "But…no, that's not right." She touched her fingers to her head. "It's getting all mixed up again."

"Her mother?" Landon questioned. "So you're positive she's not yours…ours?"

"Yes, I'm certain."

She couldn't tell if Landon was relieved about that or not. He didn't seem relieved about anything. Neither was she. The child might not be theirs, but Tessa still needed to protect the newborn.

But who was after the baby? And why?

Her gaze dropped to the baby. "I think I know the reason I have her, though. Because a killer was after her mother, and she left the baby with me for safekeeping."

"A killer," Landon said. "You mean Joel?"

"I just don't know." Tessa groaned softly. "If I could just rest for a while, maybe that would help me remember?"

"You'll get some rest later. For now, tell me what happened to the baby's mother," Landon demanded.

Tessa had no idea. But this wasn't looking good. If all of this had happened four days ago, then the mother should have come back by now. If she was able to come back, that is.

Landon cursed. "Is the mother dead or hurt?"

But before she could even attempt an answer, Dade was on the phone, and she heard him ask if there was any information on the baby's mother that would match the sketchy details she'd just given them.

"Is it possible the woman who had this baby didn't have anything to do with Emmett?" Landon pressed.

"I just don't know." She paused. "But maybe Emmett was helping me find some evidence against Joel?"

As expected, that didn't go over well with Landon. He didn't come out and say that she should have contacted him instead of Emmett, but she knew that was what he was thinking.

"But why would Emmett have been helping me?" Tessa asked.

Neither of the men jumped to answer that, maybe because they didn't have a clue, but it was Landon who finally responded. "Emmett was a DEA agent in Grand Valley, and Joel had a business there."

The memories were coming but too darn slow. She huffed and rubbed the back of her neck. Or rather she tried to do that but yanked back her hand when her fingers brushed over the sensitive skin there.

"Does it hurt?" Landon asked. He leaned closer, lifted her hair and looked for himself.

"Some." Not nearly as much as her head, though. "Why? How bad does it look?"

"It looks like a wasp sting or something. But the doctor took an X-ray. If it's something serious, he'll let us know."

Now that the drugs were partially wearing off, she tried to remember what'd happened to cause this particular injury. But nothing came. Everything was still so jumbled in her head, and that couldn't last.

There were secrets in her memories, secrets that had caused someone to try to kill her, and until she unlocked those secrets, she wouldn't be able to figure out who had sent that gunman after the baby and her.

And figure out who'd killed Emmett and why.

"Good news, *maybe*," Dade said when he finished his call. "There have been no reports of a seriously injured or dead woman who gave birth in the past week, but Josh will keep calling around and see if something turns up."

"Josh?" she asked, hoping it was someone she could trust. Of course, at the moment Tessa wasn't sure she could trust anyone.

"Our cousin," Landon explained. "He's a deputy in Silver Creek."

Like Landon. Tessa prayed this Josh was being mindful of those calls and that he didn't give away any information that could put the baby's mother in further danger. Of course, it was possible the woman was dead. Just because the cops hadn't found a body didn't mean there wasn't one.

Oh, God.

Another wave of dizziness hit her, and Tessa had to lean her head against the seat. She closed her eyes, hoping it would stop. Hoping, too, that the car would soon stop, as well.

"Where are we going?" she asked. And better yet—how soon would they be there? But the moment she asked the question, Tessa got yet another bad feeling. That feeling only increased when neither Landon nor Dade jumped to answer.

"Where?" she repeated.

"Someplace you're not going to like," Landon grumbled.

Chapter Six

Landon had told Tessa that he was taking her some-place she wouldn't like. Well, it wasn't a place where he especially wanted her to be, either, but his options were limited.

And that was why Tessa was now sleeping under his own roof.

Or at least, the roof of the guesthouse at the Silver Creek Ranch where Landon had made his temporary home. Until he could come up with other arrangements, it would be Tessa and the baby's temporary home, too. With more than a half-dozen lawmen living on the grounds, it was safer than any other place Landon could think to take them.

Landon poured himself a fourth cup of coffee, figuring he'd need a fifth or sixth one to rid him of the headache he had from lack of sleep, and checked on the baby again. She was still sacked out in the bassinet his cousins had provided. Maybe Tessa was asleep, as well, because he didn't hear her stirring in the bedroom.

Since Tessa had been the one to do the baby's

2:00 a.m. feeding, Landon had brought the infant into the living-kitchen combo area with him so that Tessa could sleep in. Of course, he'd done that with the hopes that he might get in a catnap or two on the sofa—where he'd spent the night—but no such luck. His mind was spinning with all the details of the attack. With Tessa's situation. With Emmett's murder. And despite all that mind spinning, Landon still didn't have the answers he wanted.

But maybe Tessa would.

By now, those drugs she'd been given should have worn off, and that meant maybe she would be able to tell him not only who was behind the attack at the hospital but also who'd murdered Emmett.

Landon had more coffee and checked outside. Something he'd done a lot during the night and yet another of the reasons he hadn't gotten much sleep. No signs of gunmen. Thank God. But then, the ranch hands had been told not to let anyone other than family and ranch employees onto the grounds. Maybe that would be enough to stop another attack.

However, the only way to be certain of no future attacks was to catch the person responsible. Joel, maybe. He was the obvious person of interest here, but Landon wasn't ruling out Quincy. Too bad neither Landon nor any of his lawman cousins had been able to find any evidence to make an arrest for either man.

Landon heard the two sounds at once. The baby whimpered, and Tessa moved around in the bedroom. He didn't wait for Tessa to come out. Since it was time for the baby's feeding, Landon went ahead and got the bottle from the fridge and warmed it up, just as the nanny had shown him when they'd arrived yesterday. Thankfully, there were three full-time nannies at the ranch now, so he hadn't had to resort to looking up bottle-warming instructions on the internet.

He eased the baby from the bassinet, silently cursing that his hands suddenly felt way too big and clumsy. The baby didn't seem to mind, though, and she latched on to the bottle the moment it touched her mouth.

Without the baby's fussing, it was easier for Landon to hear something else. Tessa's voice. She wasn't talking loud enough for him to pick out the words, but it seemed as if she was having a conversation with someone on the phone. The guesthouse didn't have a landline, but there was a cell phone on the nightstand for guests—something that apparently Tessa had decided to make use of. But before Landon could find out who she was calling, Tessa quit talking, and a moment later the bedroom door opened.

And there she was.

Landon hated that slam of attraction. Yeah, he felt it even now, and it was proof that attraction was more than just skin-deep. Because despite the bruises on her face, the fatigued eyes, and the baggy loaner jeans and shirt, she still managed to light fires inside him that he didn't want lit.

She opened her mouth, ready to say something, but then her attention landed on the baby. "You're feeding her," Tessa said in the same tone someone might use when announcing a miracle. Maybe because he didn't look like the bottle-feeding type.

"The nanny talked me through how to do it," he explained. "And since you'd done the other feedings, I figured it was my turn."

Tessa glanced around as if expecting to see Rose, the nanny, standing there, but the woman hadn't returned after she'd gotten them settled in the night before. That was Landon's doing.

"I didn't want to disrupt the nannies' routines any more than we already have, so I told her to go home," he explained. "My cousins have a lot of kids."

Thirteen at last count. Or maybe fourteen. Sometimes the ranch felt a little like a day care.

"I remember," Tessa said.

Two words, that was all she said, but those two words caused Landon to release the breath he didn't even know he'd been holding. Because she wasn't just talking about remembering that his cousins had plenty of children. She was talking about the memories the drugs had suppressed.

"You know who killed Emmett?" Landon asked.

His relief didn't last long, because she shook her head. "No. I don't know the person's name, but I remember what happened." Tessa lifted her shoulder. "Well, some things are still fuzzy, probably because of the drugs, but I remembered about the baby. Her name is Samantha."

"Whose child is this?" he pressed when Tessa didn't continue.

"She belongs to a friend, Courtney Hager. She

wanted me to keep the baby while she made arrangements to move. The baby's father was abusive, she said, and Courtney didn't want him anywhere near Samantha or her. She told me not to trust anyone, because the father had connections."

Landon would want to know more about those connections and the father, but for now he stood and handed Tessa the baby so he could fire off a text to his cousin Holden. Holden was a marshal and would be able to do a quick background check on this Courtney Hager. Of course, Grayson and the other deputies could do it, as well, but they were already swamped with the investigation.

In a way, Landon hated to ask Holden to do this, too. Because Emmett and Holden were brothers, and Landon knew that he and Emmett's other brothers were sick with grief over their loss. But Landon also knew that Holden and the others would do whatever it took to find Emmett's killer and that Tessa and this baby could be a connection.

"How long were you supposed to keep the baby?" Landon pressed.

"Courtney said it would only be a day or two. She's probably looking for us right now. Probably frantic, too."

Probably. Well, unless something had happened to her. "Was it Courtney you just called?"

She got that deer-caught-in-headlights look. A look that didn't please Landon one bit. "No. I called a friend," she said. "I didn't have Courtney's number memorized. It was on my cell, but I lost that somewhere in the last day or so. I wanted to try to figure out if this friend knew anything about what was going on, but he didn't answer the call."

She didn't remember Courtney's number, yet she remembered the number of this other "friend." Landon wanted to know a lot more about that, too, but it wasn't at the top of his list of questions.

"Did Courtney have anything to do with Emmett's murder?" he asked.

"No," Tessa jumped to answer. Then she paused. "But maybe her abusive boyfriend did. I don't know his name," she quickly added. "I've only known Courtney a couple of months, and I never met Samantha's father. She didn't talk about him much, but I know she's afraid of him or else she wouldn't have told me not to trust anyone."

That was something Holden might be able to uncover in the background check. Maybe this abusive guy had killed Emmett when Emmett was trying to protect the baby, though that didn't explain the note left on Emmett's body.

Tessa glanced down at the baby, brushed a kiss on her cheek. "Anything new on the attack? Did they find the gunman?" she added before he could press her for more information.

Landon would indeed press her for more, especially more about that "friend" she'd called, but for now he went with the update on the investigation. Unfortunately, he wasn't going to be the bearer of good news.

"Grayson and the deputies didn't catch the man,"

he said and paused the bottle-feeding just long enough so he could hit the button on his laptop. "It's surveillance footage from the hospital, and I want you to take a closer look. Tell me if you recognize the man who attacked us."

Maybe she would be truthful about that. Maybe.

Landon didn't look at the screen. He didn't need to, since he'd studied the footage frame by frame. Instead, he watched Tessa, looking for any signs that she knew the man who'd been trying to gun them down.

She shook her head, moved closer to the laptop. In doing so, she moved closer to Landon, her arm brushing against his. She noticed. Also noticed the scowl he gave her as a result, and Tessa inched away from him.

"I'm not positive," she said, her attention back on the screen, where she froze one of the frames, "but I think that might be the same masked man who attacked me at my house. The man who killed Emmett." Tessa pointed to the guy's hand. "See the way he's holding his gun, the way he's standing. He looks like a cop."

Could be, but Landon wasn't convinced. He could just as easily be a trained killer or a former cop.

"Who is he?" she asked.

"We still don't know. But I don't believe it's a co-incidence that Joel was there just minutes before this clown showed up."

Tessa made a sound of agreement. "Has anyone questioned Joel yet?"

"Grayson did last night. Of course, Joel claims he had nothing to do with the attack. He also came up with that name of the fire department employee who told his assistant. It was the dispatcher, Valerie Culpepper, and she confirmed she did tell the assistant."

"You believe her?"

"Not sure. Of course, it's possible Joel paid the dispatcher to say that. He could have known you were at the hospital because he or his hired gun was at the scene of the fire and saw you'd been taken away in an ambulance."

Since there was only one hospital in Silver Creek and it wasn't that big of a building, Tessa wouldn't have been hard to find.

Landon's phone buzzed, and when he saw Holden's name on the screen, he stepped away to take the call. Not that he could step far. The guesthouse wasn't that big, but he went into the living room area.

"Dade told me what happened at the hospital," Holden said the moment Landon answered. "Any reason I didn't hear it from you?"

"I've been busy. I'm with Tessa."

"Yeah. I heard that, too." Even though Holden didn't come out and say it, Landon heard the disapproval in his cousin's voice. Probably because Holden knew how Tessa had treated him. "I'm guessing Tessa's the reason you wanted me to find out about Courtney Hager?"

"She is. The baby that Tessa had with her belongs to Courtney." Landon nearly added some *maybes* in that explanation since he wasn't sure if Tessa was telling him the truth. Not the whole truth, anyway. But Holden would have automatically known that Landon had doubts about his former lover.

"I'll do a more thorough check," Holden continued a moment later, "but here's what I got. Courtney Hager is twenty-nine, unmarried and is a bookkeeper. Her address is listed in Austin."

"Have someone sent out there to do a welfare check on her," Landon suggested. That was only an hour away, but the local cops there could do that ASAP.

"She's in danger?" Holden didn't hesitate with that question.

"Possibly." And that was, sadly, the best-case scenario here. If she truly did have an abusive ex, then it was possible she was already dead. "If she's home, the locals need to take her into custody and bring her here to Silver Creek."

"Got it," Holden assured him. "What about Tessa? You want me to arrange a safe house for her?"

"Thanks, but I'm already working on it." Landon paused. "Are you...okay?"

It wasn't something he'd normally ask his cousin. Holden wasn't exactly the type to want anyone to ask that, either, but Landon wanted to make sure he wasn't pushing Holden too hard this soon after his brother's death.

"I just want to find the bastard who killed Emmett," Holden answered. "I won't be okay until then."

Landon knew exactly how Holden felt. He finished the call and turned to face Tessa.

"I'm going to a safe house?" she asked. Clearly, she'd heard the conversation.

Landon nodded. "The baby will, too. As long as the gunman's out there, you'll need protection."

She didn't disagree with that, but she made a weary sigh and sank down onto the chair. "Joel," was all she said. "It has to be him. He must have been the one who hired that guy who killed Emmett and attacked me. I've been hiding from him all these months, but he must have found me and sent a thug after me."

If Landon followed this line of reasoning, then it was also a thug who'd killed Emmett. "Do you remember why Joel would want you dead?"

She nodded, and since Samantha was finished with the bottle, Tessa put the baby against her shoulder to burp her. "I found out…something." She swallowed hard, and when her gaze met his, Landon saw the tears shimmering in her eyes. "I told you I believed Joel had murdered someone. It was a man named Harry Schuler."

The name didn't mean anything to Landon, but like Courtney, he'd soon find out everything he could about him. "How long have you known about this murder?" he asked.

"Several months."

Landon cursed. Then he bit back more profanity since it seemed wrong to curse in front of a baby. "Months? Why didn't you come to me with this? Or to anybody in law enforcement?"

"No proof. Not just about that but any of the other illegal things that I'm certain Joel was doing."

Landon was certain of those illegal things, too, and he motioned for her to continue.

"By the time Harry Schuler was killed, I'd stopped working for Joel," she went on after taking in a long breath. "But I pretended to stay friendly with Joel so I could keep digging into his business dealings."

"Define *friendly*," Landon snapped.

She flinched a little. "Nothing like that. But I didn't want Joel to know I was on to him."

"Good thing. Or he would have killed you, too. What kind of dirt did you have on Joel?"

Tessa shook her head. "Everything I found was circumstantial at best. Vaguely worded emails and part of a phone conversation I overheard. That's really why I jumped at the chance when Joel wanted me to become a PI, so I'd have the resources and contacts to look for something concrete that could be used for an arrest. I wanted to get some proof because I knew if I accused him and he didn't go to jail, that he would kill me."

Landon tried to process that while he fired off yet another text to his cousin. This time he asked Holden to get him more info on Harry Schuler.

"You said Joel wanted you to be a PI," he reminded her. "You think that's because he could use you in some way? Maybe so he could get access to those data bases you mentioned?"

"Could be, but he never asked me for any specific info from them. He only wanted me to vet potential clients to make sure they had the finances to cover whatever deal he was making with them."

But Joel was smart, and he might have been giving Tessa just enough rope to hang herself. "When specifically did this possible murder happen?"

Silence.

Oh, man. He didn't like this at all.

"That same week we slept together," she finally said. "*Before* we slept together," Tessa clarified.

That made the cut even deeper. She'd had sex with him while withholding something as huge as an alleged murder.

"If you believed Joel was capable of murder, then why leave with him that morning after you were with me?" Landon asked.

Oh.

He saw it in her eyes then. "You thought Joel would try to kill me," Landon concluded.

She nodded. "Maybe even kill both of us."

Landon had to bite back more profanity, and it took him a moment to get his jaw unclenched so he could speak. "Protecting me wasn't necessary, and it was stupid for you to go off with him like that."

"I thought if I went with him, then I'd be able to find the proof that he'd murdered Harry Schuler."

Landon jabbed his finger in her direction. "There's no argument, *none*, that you can make that'll have me agreeing with what you did." He tapped his new badge. "I'm a cop, and I could have handled this the right way."

And there was no chance she could refute that

this had been anything but the right way. Now Emmett was dead, Courtney was heaven knew where, and Tessa had a killer after her.

"I was planning to come to you," she said after several quiet moments. "I got your address in Houston and had put it in my GPS, but then the baby kept fussing, so I decided to make a detour to my house here in Silver Creek."

Landon didn't have to tell her that the second part of that wasn't such a good idea. Even though her house was in town and near the sheriff's office, someone could have been watching it.

"Is that how the gunman found you?" he asked. "Were you going to your house?"

She nodded. "I didn't see him following me until it was too late. I tried to outrun him, and that's how I ended up near the barn. The memories are sketchy after that, though. I don't have any idea how I got from my car to the barn."

Because she'd been drugged a second time, that was why. While Landon hoped she would recover all her memories, including those, recalling an attack that'd nearly left her dead wouldn't help her sleep at night. Still, the devil was in the details of those memories.

Emmett's killer was.

And anything she could tell him might help him figure out who'd sent that ski-masked thug after Emmett and her. Or if it was indeed the same thug who'd committed this crime spree.

She stayed quiet a moment, her own jaw muscles

stirring. "Tell me about that picture of the man you showed me. Quincy Nagel."

Since Landon was still trying to rein in his temper, it took him a moment to switch gears. "He's someone I arrested. And yes, it's possible he's the one who had Emmett murdered, but right now Joel is looking like my top suspect."

What he needed now was proof. And more answers. Landon thought he might get at least one of those answers on the bedroom phone that Tessa had used to call her friend.

He excused himself without telling Tessa what he was going to do, and he went into the bedroom. Landon went through the cache of recent calls, but Tessa had obviously cleared the one she'd made. There wasn't a good reason for her to do that, and he went back into the living room, ready to demand a full explanation as to what was going on. However, before he could do that, Landon's phone buzzed, and it wasn't his cousin this time.

It was Dr. Michelson.

Since it was barely 6:00 a.m. and nowhere near normal office hours, Landon figured it had to be important, so he answered it right away.

"I just got back the results of Tessa's tests," the doc said, skipping any greeting. "You need to bring her back to the hospital immediately."

Chapter Seven

Tessa couldn't stop herself from thinking the worst. Easy to think the worst after everything she'd been through. But it wasn't the memories of the attacks that troubled her most right now.

It was what she couldn't remember.

Those hours right after she'd been given the drugs were still a blur, and she needed to recall every second of what'd happened to her. Maybe then she would know who had done this to her.

"Any idea what it is?" Dr. Michelson asked Landon. They were looking at what the doctor had just extracted from her neck. It was only about a quarter of an inch long and looked like a tiny bullet.

"I think it's a tracking device," Landon answered.

Tessa's stomach dropped. To think she'd been walking around with that in for heaven knew how long, and she couldn't even remember how she'd gotten it. Of course, it wasn't very big, but she still should have known that something wasn't right, and it sickened her to think of what else this unknown monster could have done to her.

"I'll need it bagged as evidence," Landon instructed the doctor, and he glanced back at her. "You okay?"

Tessa lied with a nod, and even though Landon likely knew it was a lie, he also understood something else. It could have been much worse.

Now that she'd had a thorough exam, Tessa knew she hadn't been sexually assaulted and that her captor had given her a powerful barbiturate cocktail. She also knew that she hadn't given birth, but then, she hadn't needed an exam to confirm that. Her memories of Courtney calling her and asking her to come and get the baby were clear.

She also had clear memories of how afraid Courtney had been.

Tessa had hurried next door to Courtney's rental house when she'd heard that fear in the woman's voice, and when Courtney had begged her to take the baby for safekeeping, Tessa had done it. After she'd tried to talk Courtney into going to the authorities, that is. Courtney had flat-out refused that, though.

"Why would someone have injected Tessa with a tracking device?" the doctor asked Landon.

"Probably in case she escaped. That way her captor could find her."

Oh, God. "The baby." Tessa tried to get off the table, despite the fact the nurse was still bandaging her neck. "Someone could have used the tracking device to follow us to the ranch."

Landon motioned for her to stay down, and he made a call to the ranch, where they'd left Saman-

tha with a nanny and several of his lawman cousins. The ranch had security, but it wasn't a fortress,
and a gunman might be able to get onto the grounds
and hurt the baby.

"Everything's fine," Landon relayed after he finished his short call. "The ranch hands are all on alert,
and they'll let one of my cousins know if they see
anyone suspicious." Landon walked closer to her.
"Besides, this tracking device was on you, not the
baby."

Yes, he was right. Maybe that meant the gunman
wasn't after Samantha at all but just her. That didn't
help with the tangle of nerves she was feeling. The
newborn could be in danger all because of her.

"Will you be able to tell who was getting information from the tracking device?" she asked once
the nurse was out of the room. It wasn't that Tessa
didn't trust the woman, but she wasn't sure she fully
trusted anyone right now.

Landon lifted his shoulder. "We'll try, but it's
probably a microchip that can be tracked with a computer. It does make me wonder, though, why someone would go to the trouble of injecting you with it."

Tessa gave that some thought but had to shake her
head. She didn't know why, either, but it was obvious whoever had attacked her had wanted to be able
to find her if she escaped.

Unless…

"Maybe this person wanted me to come to you,"
she said on a rise of breath.

"I'm not a hard man to find," Landon pointed out.

"But this could mean the person didn't want you dead. Not when he or she put that tracker device on you, anyway."

True. If someone had gotten close enough to do that to her, they could have easily just killed her. Not exactly a comforting thought.

Dr. Michelson put the tracking device in a plastic bag and looked at Landon. "You want me to have Grayson or one of the other deputies pick this up?"

"No. I'll take it. When will she be free to go?"

The doctor looked at her. "She can leave now but keep an eye on her. The barbiturates have worn off, but she still could experience some dizziness."

Yes, the dizziness was there, and her head still felt a little foggy. Still, it was better than not knowing who she was. At least now she could start to look for the person behind this.

Either Landon had noticed she was wobbly or else he was just being cautious, because he took hold of her arm and helped her from the examining table. "Come on. I can drop off this tracking device at the sheriff's office, and we can give our statements about the attack."

That wasn't exactly a surprise for Tessa. She knew they needed to do the paperwork, but that meant facing yet more Ryland lawmen who wanted answers she didn't have. Even after regaining most of her memories, she didn't know who'd murdered one of their own.

With Landon's grip still firm on her arm, they made their way to the exit. Since Dade had driven with him, she expected to see him waiting in the cruiser just outside. But Tessa stopped in her tracks when she saw the scowling man. Not Dade.

But Deputy Mason Ryland.

None of the Rylands had been especially friendly to her, but Mason had a dark and dangerous edge to him, and right now he was aiming some of that intensity at her.

"Dade had to leave for a parent-teacher thing at the school," Mason growled. "I drew the short straw."

Clearly, he wasn't happy about that, but then, she'd never actually seen Mason happy. "Thank you," Tessa told him, but that only intensified the scowl.

"As soon as you drop us off at the sheriff's office, you can head back to the ranch," Landon told him Landon's eyes met hers as they got into the backseat of the cruiser. "Mason's retiring as a Silver Creek deputy. That's why Grayson offered me the job."

Tessa knew Mason pretty much ran the sprawling ranch and had done so for years, so that was probably why he was giving up his deputy duties. But she also suspected that Landon had pressed for the job. So he could catch his cousin's killer.

"Who did you call this morning?" Landon asked out of the blue. Except it probably wasn't out of the blue for him. He was like a dog with a bone when he latched on to anything to do with the investigation. And sadly, this might have something to do with it. Of course, it wouldn't be a simple explanation.

Or one that Landon would like.

"His name is Ward Strickland," she said and tried to figure out the best way to spill all of this.

"A boyfriend?" Landon didn't hesitate. He also continued to glance around, no doubt to make sure that they weren't being followed or that the gunman wasn't nearby, ready to launch another attack.

"Hardly. I haven't had a boyfriend since you." She hadn't meant to blurt that out, and it made her sound even more pathetic than she already was. Telling him about Ward wouldn't help that, either. "He's a Justice Department agent." Tessa paused. "But I'm not sure I can trust him."

She hadn't thought anyone's scowl could be worse than Mason's, but she'd been wrong. Landon beat him. "Explain that now," he demanded.

Tessa took a deep breath first. "You already know I was looking for dirt on Joel. Well, Ward said he was, too, and he contacted me to see if I had anything he could use to make an arrest. I didn't, but Ward kept hounding me to dig deeper. He wanted me to tell him anything I found out about Joel."

Landon fired off a text, no doubt to have one of his cousins run a background check on the agent. "Why aren't you sure you can trust him?" Landon asked.

"Gut feeling." She braced herself for Landon to groan. He didn't. "Once I found an email that Joel had sent. It possibly connected him to some illegal arms. *Possibly*," she emphasized. "Anyway, the day before Emmett was killed, I gave Ward a copy of the email, but a few hours later, I noticed the email had been deleted off Joel's server. I'd been checking for things like that, hoping to find something to use to have Joel arrested."

Landon stayed quiet a moment. "You think this agent could be working for Joel and just wanted to figure out if you were on to anything? Or maybe he wanted to make sure you didn't find something?"

There it was in a nutshell. "If Ward is on Joel's payroll, maybe he's the one behind the attacks."

No quiet moment this time. Landon cursed. "So why did you call him this morning? And I'm guessing it wasn't because you thought he could help you find Courtney."

"No. He doesn't know Courtney. I told you that because I didn't want to explain who he was. Not until I'd found out more about what was going on."

Landon made a circling motion with his finger to indicate he wanted this explanation to continue. He also hoped she understood that he wasn't happy with the lie she'd told him.

"I called Ward to feel him out, to try and see if he had anything to do with this. But he didn't answer. The call went straight to voice mail, so I left a message just to tell him I'd been attacked. And before you tell me that it was risky, that I could have led Ward straight to the ranch, I remember Dade saying it was a prepaid cell, so I knew Ward wouldn't be able to trace it."

More profanity from Landon, and Mason even grumbled some, as well. "If you're that worried about this guy, you should have said something before now. I'm trying to find out who came after us, and I need the names of anyone who could have been involved. *Anyone*," Landon emphasized.

Tessa couldn't argue with that. "I just didn't think you'd want to rely on my gut feelings."

"A disappearing email is more than a gut feeling," Landon verified as Mason pulled to a stop in front of the sheriff's office. "Anyone connected to Joel is a suspect."

No argument there, either. "But Joel doesn't need to hire a federal agent to come after me. I'm sure he already has plenty of hired thugs."

Landon didn't answer. In fact, he was no longer looking at her. Instead, his attention was on the two men who were entering the sheriff's office. One of the men was in a wheelchair, and the other, much larger man was helping him through the door.

"Did Grayson call him in for questioning?" Landon asked.

"No," Mason snarled. "He was going to wait until after he questioned Joel again later this morning. Maybe I should take Tessa back to the ranch while you deal with this?"

Tessa wasn't sure why Mason had said that until she got a better look at the man in the wheelchair. Landon had shown her his mug shot. Quincy Nagel.

And he was yet another suspect.

Quincy had barely made it into the office when Landon stepped from the car. Quincy turned his wheelchair in their direction, and much to Tessa's surprise, the man smiled.

"Thank God you're here," Quincy said. But he

wasn't looking at Landon when he spoke. He was looking at Tessa. "Where's the baby? I'm here to take my daughter home."

LANDON HADN'T BEEN sure what exactly Quincy would say to him, but he hadn't expected *that*.

Clearly, neither had Tessa, because she got out of the cruiser to face the man. In case this was some kind of ploy to get her out in the open so someone could gun her down, Landon hooked his arm around her and maneuvered her into the sheriff's office. Mason followed.

The place wasn't exactly quiet. Two deputies were at their desks in the open squad room, and Landon spotted Grayson in the hall outside his office. Like the deputies, he was in the middle of a phone call, but when he spotted them, he disconnected and headed for them.

"Trouble?" Grayson immediately asked.

Probably. Trouble and Quincy often went together.

"No trouble, Sheriff," Quincy insisted. He didn't sound like the thug that Landon knew he was. Didn't look like one today, either. He was wearing a dark blue suit and so was the linebacker-sized guy behind his wheelchair.

"You said something about a baby?" Tessa asked.

Quincy smiled. "Samantha. I understand you've been keeping her for Courtney."

Landon looked at her to see if this was yet something else she'd kept from him, but she looked as shell-shocked as Landon felt. That precious little girl was Quincy's?

"So where is she?" Quincy asked.

"I don't know what you're talking about," Landon said before Tessa could speak. No way was he handing over a newborn to this man.

Quincy's thin smile didn't stay in place for long. "But you do know." His jaw tightened. Eyes narrowed. "Quit playing games with me and give me my daughter. I know that Courtney gave Tessa the baby, but that's only because she couldn't find me. Well, I'm here now, so give Samantha to me."

Landon needed to stall him until he could either get in touch with Courtney or find out what the heck was going on.

"Tessa and I don't have your daughter," Landon said. "The baby we have is ours."

The squad room suddenly got very quiet. Grayson knew Landon had just lied through his teeth. Mason, too.

Quincy looked Tessa over from head to toe. "You expect me to believe that you just had a baby?"

Even though Tessa was wearing loose loaner jeans, they skimmed her body enough to show her flat stomach. But Tessa didn't panic, and she stepped right into the lie by taking hold of Landon's arm and leaning against him.

"Tessa kept the pregnancy from me," Landon added. "But she had no choice but to come to me when someone tried to kill her. What exactly do you know about that?"

Quincy shook his head as if trying to figure out what was going on, but then Landon saw the moment the man pushed his surprise aside to deal with the accusation. "Nothing. You believe I tried to hurt Tessa?"

"Did you?" Landon didn't even try to sound as if Quincy might be innocent. Plain and simple, Quincy hated him, and he hated Emmett, too, for testifying against him. That hatred could have bubbled over to Tessa.

Except Quincy might not have gone after Tessa because of any ill will he was feeling for Landon. This could indeed be connected to the baby.

"Where's Courtney?" Landon asked.

Quincy shook his head again, and Landon got a flash of the thug behind the newly polished facade. "You tell me. Are you hiding her from me?"

"Is there a reason I'd do that?" Landon countered.

Oh, Quincy did *not* like that. The anger slashed through his eyes. "You have no right. Courtney is my lover, the mother of my child. Tessa knows that."

"No, I don't," Tessa argued. "Courtney's never even mentioned you, but she did tell me that Samantha's father was abusive."

"That's a lie!" Quincy shouted. "I never laid a hand on Courtney."

The goon behind his wheelchair leaned down and whispered something to him. Landon didn't know what the guy said, but it caused Quincy to rein in his temper.

"I want my daughter, and I want her now," Quincy

insisted. "And don't say you don't have her, because I know you do."

Landon lifted his shoulder. "You're mistaken." And Landon left it at that. "Now, let's talk about Emmett. About his murder."

The rein on Quincy's temper didn't last long, and Landon could practically see the veins bulging on the man's neck. "I had nothing to do with that."

"I don't believe you. I think you killed him to get back at me."

The goon whispered something else, or rather that was what he tried to do, but this time Quincy batted him away. "You have no proof linking me to Emmett's death."

"Wrong." Landon decided to test out his latest theory. "You went to Tessa's, looking for Courtney and the baby, and Emmett was there. You got violent, Emmett tried to stop you, and you killed him."

Despite his tense muscles, Quincy managed a smile. "I didn't know you believed in fairy tales. I've never stepped foot in Tessa's place, and that means there's not a shred of physical evidence to link me to it or Emmett's murder." He made a show of gripping on to his wheelchair. "Besides, how could I overpower Emmett when I can't even walk?"

"You don't need to walk to shoot someone," Landon argued. "Or to hire a thug to shoot someone. With the trust fund your parents left you, I'm betting you've got plenty of funds to hire plenty of thugs."

"Prove it," Quincy snapped. He motioned for his goon to get him moving. "In the meantime, I'll work on getting a court order to force you to turn over my daughter to me. Neither Courtney nor you will keep her from me."

Landon considered holding Quincy for questioning, but the man would just lawyer up. It was best if Landon backed off, regrouped and figured out exactly how Quincy was involved in this.

Quincy's goon wheeled him out of the sheriff's office, but Landon didn't stand there and watch them leave. He moved Tessa away from the windows in case Quincy or his hired gun started shooting. Since Landon didn't have a private office, he took her down the hall to one of the interview rooms.

"I didn't know Quincy was involved with Courtney," Tessa said the moment they were inside. "I told the truth when I said she'd never mentioned him."

Landon believed her. "Quincy could have been lying about Courtney."

Tessa blinked. Shook her head. "But why would he do that?"

"I'm not sure." But Landon intended to find out. He took out his phone, and this time he didn't text his cousin Holden. He called him, and he put it on Speaker. Mainly because he knew Tessa would want to hear this, and he didn't want her standing too close to listen. "Please tell me you found out something, anything, about Courtney Hager."

"Bad morning?" Holden asked, probably because Landon hadn't even bothered with a greeting.

"I've had better. I just had a visit from Quincy

Nagel claiming he's the father of the baby Tessa was protecting. Courtney Hager's baby."

"Quincy, huh? Haven't found a connection between Courtney and him. Uh, can Nagel even father a child?"

"His paralysis is in his legs, so yes, I'm guessing he could. But that doesn't mean he did. What did you find out about Courtney?"

"Not much at all. She has no criminal record, and she did have a baby just last week. She also moves around a lot. I mean like every couple of months. The local cops did a welfare check for me, but she wasn't home, and her neighbors said they hadn't seen her in days."

That was possibly because she was on the run, hiding out from Quincy, but it was just as possible that she was hurt. Or dead. Quincy could have gotten to her before he came looking for his baby. If he had a baby, that is.

"Did you have DNA tests run on the baby?" Holden asked.

"Yes," Landon answered. "But I did that in case the child turned out to be mine. Now we could look for a match with Quincy, and it'll speed things up because Quincy's DNA is already in the system."

"I'll get to work on seeing if it's a match. And I'll keep looking for a connection between Quincy and her," Holden went on. "By the way, did Tessa remember anything else that could help us find Emmett's killer?"

"Nothing so far, but Grayson is questioning Joel

later this morning. I'll be here for that—after I take Tessa back to the ranch."

Tessa's gaze flew to his. "I want to be here for Joel's interview, too," she insisted.

His first reaction was to say no, that she didn't need to go another round with Joel, but if Landon had been in her place, he would have wanted to hear what the creep had to say about the attack.

"I'll let you two work that out," Holden grumbled. "If I find out anything else, I'll call you."

Landon put his phone away and stared at her. "Tell me everything you know about Courtney. How did you meet? How long have you known her?"

"Like I already told you, I've only known her a few months. She moved into the rental house next to me, and while she was waiting on her internet to be connected, she came over and asked to use mine." She paused. "I did a computer check on Courtney, to make sure she wasn't someone Joel hadn't sent over to spy on me. I didn't find anything."

Good. Because a connection to Quincy was bad enough. Still, that didn't mean this wasn't all stirred together somehow. But at the moment Landon couldn't see how. If Quincy had arranged for Courtney and Tessa to meet, what could he have gained by that? It was the same for Courtney. If the woman had known about his affair with Tessa or Landon and Quincy's bad blood, why wouldn't she have said anything about it?

Landon was still trying to piece together some answers when his phone buzzed, and he saw the name on the screen of someone who just might be able to help him with those answers.

Ward Strickland.

Tessa must have seen it, too, because she pulled in her breath. "I want to talk to him," she insisted.

"For now, just listen," Landon instructed. Whether she would or not was anyone's guess. Like his, her nerves were sky-high right now.

"Deputy Ryland," Ward said the moment Landon answered. "Your cousin Holden told me you needed to speak to me. Is this about Tessa? Do you know where she is?"

Landon took a moment to consider how to answer that. "She's in protective custody. Someone's been trying to kill her," he settled for saying.

"Yes, I heard. She left me a message but didn't give me any details. Is she all right?" The man's tone sounded sincere enough, but Landon wasn't going to trust him merely on that.

"For now. But I need proof as to who's behind these attacks. I'm hoping you can help with that."

Even from the other end of the line, Landon heard the agent's weary sigh. "I'm sure Tessa would say it's Joel."

"Is it?" Landon pressed.

"Maybe, but I've been investigating Joel for a year now, and I haven't found any evidence to arrest him for a misdemeanor, much less the felonies that Tessa claims he's been committing."

Tessa shook her head and looked ready to launch

into an argument about that, but Landon motioned for her to keep quiet.

"You believe Joel's innocent?" Landon came out and asked Ward.

"No, not totally, but I'm not sure I believe what Tessa said he did. In fact, I'm not sure I can trust Tessa."

Thankfully, Tessa didn't gasp or make a sound of outrage, though there was some anger going through her eyes.

"I need to talk to Tessa," Ward went on. "I tried to trace the call she made to me, but it came from a prepaid cell, and she didn't leave a number where she could be reached."

"You want to talk to her even if you don't trust her?" Landon snapped.

"Of course." The agent paused. "Because I'm not just investigating Joel. I'm also investigating her. I believe they're working together, or else Tessa could be using Joel as a front man for several illegal operations. Specifically, gunrunning and money laundering."

Tessa no longer looked angry. But rather defeated. Landon couldn't blame her. She'd been attacked at least three times and had been drugged, and someone had injected her with a tracking device. Now here was a federal agent accusing her of assorted felonies.

"I want to take Tessa into custody," Ward continued. "If she's truly in danger, I can protect her. And if she's helping Joel, maybe I can learn that, too. When can I pick her up?"

Landon's first instinct was to tell his guy to take a hike, but there was no sense showing Ward his hand. "I'll get back to you on that. Gotta go." And Landon ended the call.

Tessa was shaking her head before Landon even slipped his phone back into his pocket. "I'm not going with Ward. He could be trying to set me up to cover for Joel."

She turned as if to bolt out of there, but Landon took hold of her shoulders to stop her. "You're not going anywhere with Ward."

Her breath rushed out. Maybe from relief, but her eyes watered. "I'm not helping Joel," she said, her voice more breath than sound. "And I'm not a criminal."

Landon wasn't made of ice, especially around Tessa, and seeing those fresh tears in her eyes melted the ice he wished were there. Cursing himself, cursing Tessa, too, he slid his arm around her waist and eased her closer.

She melted against him. As if she belonged there.

His body seemed to think she belonged, not just in his arms. But other places. Like his bed. Still, Landon pushed that aside and tried to do what any de-iced human would do—comfort Tessa. It seemed to work, until she looked up at him.

Hell.

He didn't want another dose of this, but he wasn't exactly moving away from her, either. In fact, Landon thought he might be inching closer.

Yeah, he was.

And he didn't just inch with his body. He lowered his head, touched his mouth to hers. Now would have been a really good time for her to come to her senses and push him away. Thankfully, she did. Tessa stepped back.

"I'll bet you're already regretting that," she said, pressing her lips together a moment.

"I regretted it before I even did it." Regretted even more that it would happen again.

Landon wanted to think he could add a *probably* to that—that other kisses would probably happen— but he wasn't a man who approved of lying to himself. The *probably* was a lie. If he was around Tessa, he would kiss her again. And that was a really good reason to come up with other arrangements for her protective custody.

Definitely not Ward. But maybe he could arrange for her to stay with Holden for a while.

There was a knock at the door, and even though Tessa was no longer in his arms, she moved back even farther. The door opened, and Grayson stuck his head inside. His attention went to Tessa, not Landon.

"There's a woman lurking across the street," Grayson said. "I haven't been out there, because I didn't want to spook her, but it's possible it's Courtney."

That got Tessa moving, and Landon had to hurry to get in front of her. "I don't want you outside," Landon reminded her.

He wasn't even sure she heard him, because Tessa was already looking out the window. Landon did the same, and it didn't take him long to spot the woman. Lurking was a good description since she was in the narrow alley between two buildings, and she was glancing over at the sheriff's office.

Landon had seen Courtney's driver's license photo, but it was hard to tell if it matched this woman. The hair color was right, but she was wearing a baseball hat that she'd pulled low over her face. Also, with the baggy dark blue dress she was wearing, he couldn't tell if she had recently given birth.

"It could be her," Tessa said, shaking her head. "But I'm not sure."

"I'll go out and talk to her," Landon volunteered. "Wait here," he warned Tessa. "And I mean it."

Grayson stepped beside her and gave Landon a glance to assure him that Tessa was staying put. Good. One less thing to worry about.

Landon went outside, but he didn't make a beeline toward the woman. If this was Courtney, then she probably wouldn't trust him just because he was a cop. He first wanted to make sure it was her, and then he could try to coax her into going inside.

But the woman surprised Landon by calling out to him. "Are you Landon Ryland, the cop Tessa told me about?" she asked.

"I am." Landon went a little closer, wishing he could get a better look at her face.

And he did.

The woman moved out from the alley, not onto the sidewalk but just enough for him to see her.

Hell.

It wasn't Courtney. Landon didn't have a clue who she was, but when she lifted her hand, he saw the gun.

The gun she pointed right at him.

Chapter Eight

Tessa got just a glimpse of the woman taking aim at Landon before Grayson shoved her behind him.

"Get down!" Tessa managed to shout to Landon. But it was already too late.

The woman fired at him.

Landon dropped down, and the bullet slammed into the window. The glass was reinforced, so the shot didn't go through into the squad room, but Landon wasn't behind the glass. He was out there in the open.

Oh, God.

It was happening again. Someone was trying to kill them, and Landon was in danger because of her.

It was hard for Tessa to see around Grayson, and it got even harder when the other two deputies stepped up, as well. All three of them took aim, but it was Grayson who stepped out. He delivered a shot that had the woman ducking back into the alley, and the sheriff continued to shoot at her until Landon could scramble back inside.

"It's not Courtney," Landon relayed to her.

Tessa heard him, but she couldn't respond, because she had to make sure he wasn't hurt. There'd been a lot of shots fired, but Landon appeared to be unharmed.

And riled to the core.

"I don't want her to get away," Landon growled. "I'll go out back and see if I can get her in my line of sight."

"I'll do it," Grayson insisted. "In the meantime, take Tessa to my office. This could be some kind of trap."

Tessa hadn't even thought of that, but he was right. There were four lawmen in the building, and their instincts were no doubt to go in pursuit of the shooter. That might be exactly what their attacker wanted, and he could use this to come after Tessa again. Still, she didn't want Grayson hurt, either.

"Be careful," Tessa called out as the sheriff and one of the other deputies hurried toward the back exit.

Landon didn't waste any time taking her to Grayson's office, but he didn't go inside with her. He stayed in the hall with his gun ready while he volleyed glances at both the front and back of the building.

Another shot.

But Tessa didn't know if the woman had fired it or if it was Grayson.

"She wanted us to think she was Courtney," Tessa said, thinking out loud.

"Yeah. I believe she was sent here to draw you out."

And it'd nearly worked. If Landon hadn't held her back, Tessa would have indeed gone out there. But which of their suspects would be most likely to use a Courtney look-alike to do that?

Quincy Nagel.

Plus, the man had just left the building, so he could be out there somewhere watching his "handiwork." It sickened her to think of Courtney being involved with a man like that. Sickened her even more that Quincy might have already found Courtney and killed her.

"Hell," Landon growled. "I don't need this now."

Tessa could see why he'd said that, but it sent her heart pounding, and a moment later she heard a voice she didn't want to hear. Joel.

"What the hell's going on?" Joel spat out.

She heard some kind of struggle, maybe between Joel and the deputy, but Landon didn't budge. However, he did take aim in that direction, and every muscle in his body was primed for a fight.

"Keep your hands where I can see them," Landon ordered, and a moment later Joel scrambled into the hallway. He dropped down onto the floor, his back against the wall.

"If you demand a man come in for an interrogation," Joel snapped, "then you should make sure the place is safe first. Who the hell is shooting?"

"I thought you might know something about that," Landon countered. Now he was including Joel in those volleyed glances, and the man who crawled to Joel's side. His lawyer, no doubt.

Tessa knew that Joel was indeed coming in for an interview, and judging from the timing of the attack, this could make him appear innocent. Appear. But it was just as likely that Joel had orchestrated it just for that reason. If so, it was still risky since Joel could have been hit by a stray bullet.

More shots came.

These didn't seem as close as the others, but they still sliced through Tessa as if they'd been fired at her. Then everything stopped, and she held her breath, waiting and praying.

"Grayson's coming back," Landon relayed to her, but he still didn't budge. He stayed in front of her like a sentry.

Tessa managed to get a glimpse of Joel to see how he was dealing with this, but he was checking his phone. Obviously, being caught in the middle of an attack hadn't caused him to go into the panic mode, which only supported her notion that he could have set all of this in motion.

"I had to shoot her," she heard Grayson say. "She's dead." He didn't sound any happier about that than Landon was, and Tessa knew why. A dead shooter couldn't give them any answers.

"Get into the interview room and close the door," Landon told Joel and the lawyer, and he didn't say anything else until they had done that. "Did she say anything?" he added.

Grayson joined them in the hall, and he shook his head. "She had no ID on her, but she did have a phone. Josh is looking at it now."

Good. Maybe they'd find something to tell them who she was and who had hired her. Maybe.

Grayson tipped his head to the interview room. "Let Joel know it's going to be a while before I can talk to him. Then, you can go ahead and get Tessa out of here if you want."

She could see the debate Landon was having with himself about that. He no doubt wanted to be part of this investigation, but that wouldn't happen if he was with her at the ranch.

"As long as the baby's safe, I'll be okay here for a while longer," she offered.

"My cousins will call if there's a problem at the ranch," he said. Landon looked at the interview room. "But now that Quincy and Joel both know you're here, this is probably the last place you should be."

Ironic because it was a sheriff's office, but Tessa could see his point. As long as she was in danger, so were Landon and his cousins.

He went across the hall and opened the door of the interview room. Joel and his lawyer were huddled together, talking, but they hushed the moment Landon stepped in.

"You're going to have to wait for the interview," Landon insisted. He certainly didn't offer Joel the opportunity to reschedule.

"Who fired those shots?" Joel asked. "And don't bother accusing me, because I didn't do it. Nor did I hire someone. Was it Quincy Nagel?"

Because she was standing so close to Landon,

she felt his muscles go stiff. Tessa was certain some of her muscles did the same thing. She stepped in the doorway next to Landon so she could face Joel.

"How do you know Quincy?" Landon asked, taking the question right out of her mouth.

Joel looked as if he was fighting a smile. "Really? You don't think I've made it my business to learn everything I can about both Tessa and you? I know you crossed paths with Quincy, and I know he wants to get back at you. I saw him and some guy in a suit just seconds before the shots started. Why was he here?"

"As you said, he wants to get back at me," Landon answered. Not exactly the truth, but she didn't want to discuss Quincy's possible paternity with Joel. "What'd you learn about Quincy?"

Joel stared at him as if trying to figure out if this was some kind of trick. It wasn't, but it was a fishing expedition.

"I know you arrested him," Joel finally answered, "that he's paralyzed because of a prison fight. But I have no idea if he's the one who murdered Emmett."

"Anything else?" Landon pressed.

Joel did more staring. "What are you looking for on Quincy?"

"You tell me."

Joel chuckled. "It must make your hand really tired, holding your cards so close to the vest like that. Well, no need. I really don't know anything about Quincy."

Landon made a sound to indicate he didn't buy that. Neither did Tessa. Joel knew something…but what? Tessa would have definitely pressed for more, but from the corner of her eye, she saw Grayson motioning for them. Landon shut the door of the interview room and headed toward his cousin.

"We might have found something," Grayson said the moment they joined him. "Josh looked through the shooter's recent calls, and there's a name you'll recognize."

Tessa figured Grayson was about to say Joel's or Quincy's name. But no.

Grayson lifted the phone and showed them the screen, and Tessa had no trouble seeing the name of the caller.

Agent Ward Strickland.

WAITING HAD NEVER been Landon's strong suit, and this time was no different. Where the hell was Ward Strickland and why wasn't the agent returning Landon's calls? One way or another, he would find out why, but for now he had to wait it out.

Along with keeping Tessa and the baby safe.

That was the reason he'd brought Tessa back to the ranch, but at the time he'd done that, Landon had thought it would be only a couple of hours, but here it was nearly nightfall, and they still had nothing.

Tessa stared at him from over the dinner that the cook had brought from the main house. Fried chicken, some vegetables and homemade bread. Landon had eaten some of it. Tessa, too. But judging from the way she was picking at her food, her appetite was as off as his. Nearly being killed could do that.

"You think Ward could be dead?" she asked.

Landon had gone over all the possibilities, and yeah, that was one of them. The person behind this could have set up Ward with that phone call to the dead shooter and then murdered Ward. Without a body, it would certainly look as if Ward was guilty. And maybe he was. But Landon wanted to make sure. Tessa's and the baby's safety depended on it.

As if on cue, Samantha stirred in the bassinet. Since she'd probably want another bottle soon, Landon figured she'd wake up and start fussing, but she went back to sleep.

"So how long do we stay here?" Tessa asked.

Good question. Landon had gone over all the possibilities and for now had put the safe house on hold.

"I figured we'd need at least one of my cousins to go with us to a safe house, and that would mean tying up a deputy, one Grayson will need," he explained. "At least by being at the ranch, the hands can help with security."

She nodded but didn't look especially pleased about that. Maybe because she just felt as if she were in hostile territory here because of her connection to Emmett's death. Or maybe it was him.

Or rather that stupid kiss.

Their gazes met, and Landon knew which one it was. Definitely the kiss. Clearly, Tessa wasn't any more comfortable with the attraction than he was, because she looked away and stood. Too bad Landon did the same thing at the exact same time, and in the small space they nearly bumped into each other.

The corner of Tessa's mouth lifted in a short-lived half smile. "It's a good thing we don't have time for this," she said in a whisper.

If he'd wanted to be a jerk, he could have asked her what she was talking about, but Landon knew. It was the attraction—the reason that kiss had happened. And she was right. They didn't have time for "this."

He had things he could be doing to try to move the investigation along. Calls to make. Of course, none of those calls had resulted in anything so far, but now that they'd finished eating, he needed to get back to it. So far, they'd yet to find a number for Courtney. There wasn't a phone in her name anyway, but she could have been using a prepaid cell.

But he didn't get back to the calls.

Like in the sheriff's office, his feet seemed anchored to the floor, and he couldn't take his eyes off Tessa. What else was new? He'd always had that trouble around her, but unlike at the sheriff's office, Landon didn't pull her to him. Didn't kiss her. Instead, he took out his phone to start those calls, but before he could make the first one to Grayson, there was a knock at the door.

Landon automatically put his hand over his gun, but when he looked out the window, he realized it wasn't a threat. It was his cousin Lieutenant Nate Ryland, a cop in the San Antonio PD, and he wasn't alone. He had four kids with him. The oldest, Kimmie, was Nate's eight-year-old daughter, but the other three were Nate's nieces and nephew.

"Supplies," Nate said after Landon opened the door. He had two plastic bags, one with disposable diapers and the other containing formula.

"And a dolly for the baby," Kimmie added. She held up a curly-haired doll for Landon to see.

The four kids came in ahead of Nate and made a beeline for the bassinet. Tessa stepped back as if clearing the way, or maybe she was just alarmed by the sudden onset of chattering, running kids. Her nerves probably weren't all that steady yet, and Landon wasn't even sure she had much experience being around children.

Kimmie looked in at the baby, putting the doll next to the bassinet, but one of the other girls, Leah—at least, Landon thought it was Leah—hurried to him and hugged him. Since Leah and her twin sister, Mia, were only six years old, that meant the little girl ended up hugging his legs. Landon scooped her up and kissed her cheek.

"Are all these your children?" Tessa asked Nate.

Nate smiled. "Just that one." He pointed to Kimmie, who had her face right against Samantha's. "The boy is Grayson's son, Chet. He's five. And the twins belong to my brother Kade and his wife, Bree."

"And Uncle Landon," Leah corrected, snuggling against Landon. Landon was her cousin, not her uncle, but since Nate had five brothers, Landon figured the kids gave the uncle label to any adult Ryland male.

"Yep. I'm yours," Landon agreed, and that seemed to surprise Tessa, too. Or maybe the surprise was just because he was smiling. Landon certainly hadn't done much of that in the past couple of weeks.

"Can we keep her?" Chet asked, looking down at Samantha.

Nate didn't jump to answer, which meant he probably didn't know the situation. He knew that Samantha wasn't Landon's daughter, of course, but with the baby's mother missing, it was possible she might be at the ranch for a while.

"Don't you have enough cousins?" Nate teased the boy. He ruffled his dark brown hair.

Chet shook his head. "I don't have a sister. Once I get a brother or sister, it'll be enough."

"You'll need to talk to your mom and dad about that. Grayson and his wife, Eve, are thinking about adopting since they can't have any more children of their own," Nate added to Tessa.

Landon set Leah back down on the floor so she, too, could go see the baby, and once all four kids were gathered around the bassinet, Nate went closer to Landon and Tessa.

"I got a call from the crime lab a few minutes ago," Nate said, and he kept his voice low. Probably so the kids wouldn't hear. "Grayson asked me to try to cut through some red tape so he could get the baby's DNA test results and the tracking device the doctor took from Tessa. It's not good news on either front."

Tessa groaned softly. "Is Samantha Quincy's baby?"

"The results aren't back on that yet, but Quincy does have a fairly rare blood type, and it matches Samantha's."

Yeah, definitely not good. "Quincy said he was going to get a court order," Landon told Nate.

Nate nodded. "He's already started proceedings. Of course, his record won't work in his favor, but since he's served his time, a judge probably wouldn't block a demand for custody. That's why Grayson's pushing so hard to find the baby's mother. Still no sign of her, though."

Hell. It sickened Landon to think of Quincy getting anywhere near the newborn, much less taking her. If Courtney was still alive, Quincy could use the baby to force her to come back to him.

"What about the microchip taken from Tessa?" Landon asked.

"It's not traceable. There were thousands of them made, and the techs can't work out who, if anyone, was even monitoring it." Nate paused. "Though I'm guessing someone was monitoring it and that's how Tessa ended up in that burning barn."

Tessa made a sound of agreement. "And I don't remember who did that to me. In fact, I still don't remember much about the hours after the two times I was drugged."

That was too bad, but the doctor had already

warned Landon that those memories might be lost for good.

"Are you two, uh, back together?" Nate came out and asked.

"No," Tessa said even faster than Landon.

Maybe it was the fast answers. Maybe their body language was giving off some signs of the attraction. Either way, Nate just flexed his eyebrows.

"All right, kids, let's go," Nate said.

That got varied reactions. The twins were already bored with the baby, probably because they had a baby sister of their own at home, but Chet lingered a couple of extra seconds.

"Can't we wait until she wakes up?" Kimmie begged.

"Afraid not. I gotta get ready for work, but maybe you can come back in the morning with Uncle Mason when he stops by."

Despite Mason being the most unfriendly looking guy in the state, that pleased Kimmie. Probably because she had her uncle Mason wrapped around her little finger.

Landon got hugs from all four of them, but just as he was seeing them out, his phone buzzed, and he saw Grayson's name on the screen. Landon looked up while he answered it.

"We found Ward," Grayson greeted, but Landon could tell from the sheriff's tone that this wasn't good news. "Someone ran his car off the road, and he's banged up. He said he spent most of the afternoon at the hospital and that's why he didn't answer his phone."

"Could his injuries have been self-inflicted?" Tessa immediately asked. Landon hadn't put the call on Speaker, but she was close enough to hear.

"Possibly. I'll ask him about that when he comes in for questioning in the morning." Grayson paused. "But you should know that Ward is saying that Tessa's responsible, that she hired the person who tried to kill him." Another pause. "Ward is demanding that I arrest her."

Chapter Nine

Tessa's nerves were still raw and right at the surface, and walking into the sheriff's office didn't help. Neither would coming face-to-face with Ward, since he was accusing her of a serious crime that could lead to her arrest. Still, she wanted to confront him, wanted to try to get to the truth. But there was a problem with that.

Landon.

He didn't want her anywhere near Ward when the agent was being questioned. It had taken some doing for Tessa to talk him into allowing her to go with him and that had been only after she'd agreed she wouldn't take part in the interrogation. However, she would be able to listen and she was hoping Landon could convince Ward that she'd had no part in running him off the road.

"Move fast," Landon reminded her the moment they stepped from his truck.

He'd parked it directly in front of the sheriff's office, so it was only a few steps outside, but considering the hired gun had fired those shots just the day before, with each step, she felt as if she were in a combat zone. No way would Tessa mention that, though, since Landon was no doubt leaning toward the idea of having someone escort her back to the ranch so she could stay with the baby, his lawman cousins and the rest of his family. They'd left the baby with Mason and the nanny, and while she didn't want them to be inconvenienced for too long, this meeting was important.

"Is Ward here yet?" Landon asked Grayson the moment they were inside. Landon also moved her away from the window. Not that he had to do much to make that happen, since Tessa had no plans to stand anywhere near the glass.

Grayson nodded. "Ward's in the interview room. He still wants you arrested for hiring the person who ran him off the road," he added to Tessa.

Tessa had figured Ward wouldn't have a change of heart about that, but she had to shake her head. "Has he said why he believes I did that?"

"Not yet, but he's claiming he has proof."

Since Tessa knew she was innocent, there was no proof. But Ward might believe he had something incriminating.

"Well, we have proof of his connection to the dead woman who tried to kill us," Landon countered.

But there was something in Grayson's expression that indicated otherwise. "We checked the phone records. Ward didn't answer the call from her."

Tessa groaned because she knew that meant Ward

could claim not only that he didn't know the woman but also that the call had been made to set him up.

And it was possible that was true.

Heck, it was possible that the same person was trying to set up both of them. Joel maybe? Or Quincy? Tessa knew why Joel or even Quincy might want to set her up, but what she needed to find out was if and how Ward was connected to this.

"Quincy's lawyer has been pestering us this morning," Grayson went on. "He's trying to find a judge who'll grant him temporary custody."

Landon cursed under his breath. "Then I need to find a judge who'll block his every move." He tipped his head to the interview room. "Speaking of our sometimes-warped legal system, did Ward manage to get a warrant for Tessa's arrest?"

Grayson shook his head. "But he claims he's working on it."

"I am," someone said.

Ward.

The lanky sandy-haired agent was standing in the doorway of the interview room and stepped into the hall. His attention stayed nailed to her.

It didn't surprise her that Ward had heard Landon and her talking with Grayson. In fact, he'd no doubt been listening for her to arrive so he could confront her with the stupid allegation that she'd tried to kill him.

"Tessa," Ward greeted, but it wasn't a friendly tone.

He walked closer. Or rather he limped closer. In

addition to the limping, there was also a three-inch bandage on the left side of his forehead and a bruise on his cheek. It was obvious he'd been banged up, but Tessa figured she beat him in the banged-up-looking department.

Grayson tipped his head to the interview room. "You and I will go back in there and get started."

But Ward didn't budge. "Why do you want me dead?" he asked Tessa.

"I could ask you the same thing," she countered. It was obvious that neither Grayson nor Landon wanted her to confront Ward, but Tessa couldn't stop herself.

Ward scowled at her. "If I'd wanted you dead, I wouldn't have hired some idiot gunwoman who just happened to be carrying a phone that she used to call me. Lots of people know my phone number. Even you."

That was true, but that didn't mean Ward was innocent. It could have been a simple mistake, or else done as a sort of reverse psychology.

"Why do you think I'm trying to kill you?" Tessa asked.

Ward glanced at Landon. Then Grayson. "That was something I'd planned on telling the Texas Rangers. I figure the Silver Creek lawmen are a little too cozy with you to make sure justice is served."

Landon stepped closer, and he had that dangerous look in his eyes. "I always make sure justice is served," he snarled. "And you'd better rein in your accusations when it comes to me, Tessa and anyone else in this sheriff's office."

The anger snapped through Ward's eyes, and she could tell he wanted to challenge that. But he wasn't in friendly territory here, and he was indeed throwing out serious accusations that Tessa knew he couldn't back up.

"Let's take this to the interview room," Grayson said, and it wasn't a suggestion. He sounded just as dangerous as Landon.

"You're not joining us?" Ward asked when she didn't go any farther than the doorway.

While she wanted to know answers, she didn't want to compromise the interrogation that could possibly help them learn about a killer. "I just want to hear whatever proof you claim to have against me."

Ward didn't say anything, but he took out his phone and pressed a button. It didn't take long for the recorded voice to start pouring through the room.

"Tessa Sinclair can't be trusted," the person said. "She paid my friend to try to kill you."

That was it, all of the message, and the voice was so muffled that Tessa couldn't even tell if it was a man or a woman. But it didn't matter. Someone was trying to frame her.

"Is there any proof to go along with that?" Grayson asked, taking the question right out of her mouth.

Ward's face tightened. "No. And the call came from a prepaid cell that couldn't be traced."

Even though Tessa already knew there wouldn't be real proof, the relief flooded through her. "Someone's trying to set us up."

"Why would you think Tessa had done something like this?" Landon asked as soon as she'd finished speaking.

Ward lifted his shoulder. "I figured it was all connected. Emmett's murder. Joel. And what with Tessa being involved with Joel—"

"I wasn't involved with him," Tessa interrupted. "At least, not involved in the way you're making it sound. I was trying to find proof to send him to jail. So was Emmett. That's why he was at my house the night someone killed him."

Ward shifted his attention to Landon. "And that someone left that note tying you to the murder?"

Landon just nodded, but Tessa could tell from the way his back straightened that the connection not only sickened him but was also the reason he'd moved back to Silver Creek.

"What do you know about Quincy Nagel?" Landon asked.

Ward just stared at him. "He's involved in this?"

Landon stared at Ward, too. "I asked first."

Ward clearly didn't care for Landon's tone, but Tessa didn't care for Ward's hesitation on what was a fairly simple question.

"Word on the street is that Quincy wants to get back at you for arresting him. He blames you for being paralyzed." Ward paused again. "But I don't know whether or not he's connected to any of this." He huffed and scrubbed his hand over his face. "In fact, I don't know what the hell is going on."

Tessa felt relief about that, too. At least he wasn't yapping about trying to have her arrested.

"I'm shaken up, I guess," Ward went on a moment later. But then there was more of that anger in his eyes when he looked at her. "Swear to me that you didn't have anything to do with trying to kill me."

This was an easy response for her. "I swear. Now I want you to do the same. That gunwoman fired shots into the building. I don't want Landon or anyone else hurt because you're gunning for me."

Ward huffed. "And why exactly do you think I'd be gunning for you?"

Tessa took a couple of moments to figure out the best way to say this, but there was no best way. "I thought you could be working with Joel."

A burst of air left Ward's mouth. Definitely not humor but surprise. "Not a chance."

"Ditto," Tessa countered. "I don't work for him, either."

The silence came, and so did the stares, and it didn't sit well between them. Tessa could almost feel the tension smothering her. It helped, though, when Landon's arm brushed against hers. She wasn't even sure it was intentional until she glanced up at him.

Yes, it was intentional.

Soon, very soon, they were going to have to deal with this unwanted attraction between them.

"Did your memory return?" Ward asked her.

The question was so abrupt that it threw her for a moment. "How did you know I'd lost it?"

"Word gets out about that sort of thing. Did you remember everything?" Ward pressed.

Everything but what mattered most to Landon—who'd murdered Emmett.

"My memory is fine," Tessa settled for saying, and she watched Ward's reaction.

At least, she would have watched for it if he hadn't dodged her gaze. "And the baby that was with you when Landon rescued you from that burning barn? How is she?"

Tessa decided it was a good time to stay quiet and wait to see where he was going with this. It was possible Ward thought she had indeed given birth, because they'd mainly dealt with each other over the phone and it'd been months since she'd seen him in person.

"The baby's okay, too," Landon answered.

Ward volleyed glances between them, clearly expecting more, but neither Landon nor she gave him anything else. If they admitted the baby wasn't theirs, the word might get back to Quincy. She didn't want him to have any more fodder for trying to get custody of the baby.

Ward's glances lasted a few more seconds before he turned his head toward Grayson. "Could we get on with this interview? I also want to read Tessa's statement on the attacks."

"We're still processing the statement," Grayson volunteered.

Since Tessa had made one the night before, she doubted there was any processing to do, but she was thankful that Grayson seemed to be on her side. About this, anyway.

Landon put her hand on her back to get her moving. Not that he had to encourage her much. Tessa figured she'd personally gotten everything she could get from Ward.

"You believe him?" Landon asked. "Do you trust him?" he amended. He didn't take her back into the squad room but rather to the break room at the back of the building.

"No to both. I believe he could have been set up with that phone call from the gunwoman. Just as someone set me up with that phone call to him. But I'm not taking him off our suspect list."

Our.

She hadn't meant to pause over that word, and it sounded, well, intimate or something. Still, Landon and she had been working together, so the *our* applied.

"I should call the ranch and check on the baby," she said. She'd already walked on enough eggshells today, and besides, she did want to check on Samantha.

Landon took out his phone, made the call and then put it on Speaker when Mason answered. "Anything wrong?" Mason immediately asked.

"Fine. We're just making sure Samantha is okay."

"Yeah, I figured that's why you were calling. Are you sure you aren't the parents? Because you're acting like the kid is yours."

Landon scowled. "I'm sure. And just drop the subject and don't make any other suggestions like you did last night."

She couldn't be sure, but she thought maybe Mason chuckled. She had to be wrong about that. Mason wasn't the chuckling type.

"Quincy's not backing off the custody suit," Landon explained. "He's the kind of snake who'd try to sneak someone onto the ranch to steal the baby."

"The hands have orders to shoot at any trespassers—even one who happens to be in a wheelchair."

"Good. Tessa and I won't be much longer, and we'll head back to the ranch as soon as Grayson finishes his chat with Ward."

Landon ended the call, but as he was putting his phone away, his gaze met hers. "What?" he asked.

Tessa hadn't realized she was looking puzzled, but she apparently was. "What suggestions did Mason make?" But the moment she asked it, Tessa wished she could take it back, because Landon looked even more annoyed than he had when Mason had brought it up.

"Mason thinks you and I are together again," Landon finally said.

Tessa wasn't sure how to feel about that. Embarrassed that Mason had picked up on the attraction or worried that what she felt for Landon—what she'd always felt for him—was more than just mere attraction.

"He suggested…" But Landon stopped, waved it off. "He suggested, since it already looks as if we're together, that we should raise the baby. If Quincy is the father, that is, but isn't granted custody."

She figured Mason had suggested a little more

than that. Maybe like Landon and her becoming lovers again. Which was the last thing Landon wanted. She hadn't heard any part of his conversation with his cousin, because he'd stepped outside the guest cottage to take the call, but now Tessa wished she'd listened in.

But then she was the one to mentally wave that off.

She didn't need to be spinning any kind of fantasies about Landon, even ones that included the baby's future.

"That kiss shouldn't have happened," Landon said, and his tone indicated it wouldn't happen again. It did, though.

Almost.

He brushed a kiss on her forehead, and his mouth lingered there for a moment as if it might continue. But then they heard something that neither of them wanted to hear.

Joel.

"I have to see Landon and Tessa now," Joel practically shouted. "It's an emergency."

Mercy. What now?

Landon cursed again, and he stepped in front of her as they made their way back to the squad room. Considering the volume and emotion in Joel's voice, Tessa halfway expected to see the man hurt and bleeding. Maybe the victim of another attack. Or the victim of something staged to look like an attack. There didn't appear to be a scratch on Joel, though.

"What do you want?" Landon snarled, and he

didn't sound as if he wanted to hear a word the man had to say.

Joel went toward them. His breath was gusting, and he held out his phone. At first Tessa couldn't tell what was on the screen, but as Joel got closer, she saw the photo of the woman.

Oh, God.

"That's Courtney," she said, snatching the phone from Joel.

Now, here was someone who looked hurt and bleeding, and Courtney's blond hair was in a tangled mess around her face.

A face etched with fear.

"Look at what she's holding," Joel insisted, stabbing his index finger at the screen.

But Joel hadn't needed to point out the white sign that Courtney had gripped in her hands. Or the two words that were scrawled on the sign.

Help me.

Chapter Ten

Landon groaned and motioned for Dade to have a look at the picture Joel had just shown them.

"You're sure that's the missing woman?" Dade asked Tessa.

"I'm sure it's Courtney," Tessa answered, though she had to repeat it for her response to have any sound. She was trembling now, and some of the color had drained from her face. "Where is she? How did you get that picture?"

The questions were aimed at Joel, and Landon was about to put the guy in cuffs when he shook his head. "I don't know who or where she is," Joel insisted. "Someone texted me that picture about twenty minutes ago."

Hell. Twenty minutes was a lifetime if Courtney truly did need someone to help her. Landon hoped that *if* wasn't an issue and that the woman wasn't faking this.

"That looks like the bridge on Sanderson's Road," Dade said after he studied the photo a moment.

It did, though it'd been years since Landon had

been out there. There were two routes that led in and out of town, and Sanderson's Road wasn't the one that most people took.

"I'll call in Gage and Josh to head out there now," Dade added. He took out his phone and stepped away.

Joel moved as if to step away, as well, but Landon grabbed him by the arm. "Who's the *someone* who texted you that picture?"

"I don't know. Whoever it was blocked the number."

Landon would still have the lab check Joel's phone to see if there was some way to trace it. Or maybe there was even some way to figure out who'd taken the picture. It clearly wasn't a selfie, because he could see both of Courtney's hands, but whoever had snapped the shot was standing close to her.

"Why would someone text you about Courtney?" Tessa asked.

Joel lifted his hands in the air. "None of this makes sense, but what I don't want you doing is blaming the messenger. I did the right thing by bringing you this photo, and I don't want to be blamed for anything."

Landon would reserve blame for later, but Joel could be just as much of a snake as he was a messenger.

Dade finished his call and motioned for Landon to step into Grayson's office with him. Since Landon didn't want Tessa left alone with Joel, he took her with him.

"Gage said someone was spotted near the fence at the ranch," Dade explained.

That didn't help the color return to Tessa's face, and Landon had to step in front of her to keep her from bolting.

"The baby's okay," Dade assured her. "Everyone is. The person ran when one of the hands confronted him, but all of this is starting to feel like a trap."

Landon made a sound of agreement. "Have Josh and Gage stay put at the ranch. I'll get Joel and Ward out of here, and then while Grayson stays with Tessa, you and I can go look for Courtney."

Tessa was shaking her head before he even finished. "Courtney won't trust you. If I go with you, maybe we can get her out of there."

Now it was Landon's turn to shake his head. "You're not going out there."

"I agree," Dade said and then looked at Landon. "But I don't think you should go, either. The two of you are targets. I'll call in the night deputies, and Grayson and I can go after Courtney."

His cousin didn't wait for him to agree to that. Probably because Dade knew he was right. He went to the interview room to fill in Grayson, and Landon returned to the squad room to tell Joel to take a hike. But it wasn't necessary.

Because Joel was already gone.

Normally, Landon would have preferred not having Tessa around a creep like Joel, but it gave him an uneasy feeling that the man had just run out like that.

"I demand to know what's going on," Landon

heard Ward say. "Someone's trying to kill me, and I need to know everything about this investigation."

"We'll fill you in when we know something," Grayson said. "Now leave. I'll have someone call you and reschedule the interview."

Ward came out of the interview room, but he didn't head for the exit. He stopped in front of Landon and Tessa. "Tell me what's going on." Then he huffed, and Landon could see the man trying to put a leash on his temper. "I can help," he added as if they would agree to that.

They didn't.

Landon didn't want help from one of their suspects.

"Just go," Landon insisted.

Ward glanced at Tessa. Why, Landon didn't know. She certainly wasn't going to ask him to hang around, and while mumbling some profanity, Ward finally turned and stormed out.

Almost immediately Tessa's gaze started to fire around the room. No doubt looking for something she could do to help save her friend. Or at least, the woman she thought was her friend. As far as Landon was concerned, the jury was still out on that.

"Courtney's alive," Landon assured Tessa. "Hang on to that."

She shook her head. "Courtney was alive when that photo was taken. Just because someone sent it to Joel twenty minutes ago, doesn't mean that's when it was taken."

FREE Merchandise is 'in the Cards' for you!

Dear Reader,

We're giving away FREE MERCHANDISE!

Seriously, we'd like to reward you for reading this novel by giving you **FREE MERCHANDISE** worth over **$20** retail. And no purchase is necessary!

You see the Jack of Hearts sticker above? Paste that sticker in the box on the Free Merchandise Voucher inside. Return the Voucher today... and we'll send you Free Merchandise!

Thanks again for reading one of our novels—and enjoy your Free Merchandise with our compliments!

Pam Powers

Pam Powers

P.S. Look inside to see what Free Merchandise is **"in the cards"** for you!

W

e'd like to send you two free books like the one you are enjoying now. Your two books have a combined price of over $10 retail, but they are yours to keep absolutely FREE! We'll even send you 2 wonderful surprise gifts. You can't lose!

REMEMBER: Your Free Merchandise, consisting of **2 Free Books** and **2 Free Gifts**, is worth over $20 retail! No purchase is necessary, so please send for your Free Merchandise today.

Get TWO FREE GIFTS!

We'll also send you 2 wonderful FREE GIFTS (worth about $10 retail), in addition to your 2 Free books!

Visit us at:

www.ReaderService.com

Books received may not be as shown.

FREE MERCHANDISE VOUCHER

2 FREE BOOKS and 2 FREE GIFTS

Please send my Free Merchandise, consisting of
2 Free Books and **2 Free Mystery Gifts**.
I understand that I am under no obligation to buy
anything, as explained on the back of this card.

❏ I prefer the regular-print edition
182/382 HDL GLUX

❏ I prefer the larger-print edition
199/399 HDL GLUX

Please Print

FIRST NAME

LAST NAME

ADDRESS

APT.#   CITY

STATE/PROV.   ZIP/POSTAL CODE

NO PURCHASE NECESSARY!

I-N16-FMC15

READER SERVICE—Here's how it works:

Accepting your 2 free Harlequin Intrigue® books and 2 free gifts (gifts valued at approximately $10.00) places you under no obligation to buy anything. You may keep the books and gifts and return the shipping statement marked "cancel." If you do not cancel, about a month later we'll send you 6 additional books and bill you just $4.74 each for the regular-print edition or $5.49 each for the larger-print edition in the U.S. or $5.49 each for the regular-print edition or $6.24 each for the larger-print edition in Canada. That is a savings of at least 11% off the cover price. It's quite a bargain! Shipping and handling is just 50¢ per book in the U.S. and 75¢ per book in Canada.* You may cancel at any time, but if you choose to continue, every month we'll send you 6 more books, which you may either purchase at the discount price plus shipping and handling or return to us and cancel your subscription. *Terms and prices subject to change without notice. Prices do not include applicable taxes. Sales tax applicable in N.Y. Canadian residents will be charged applicable taxes. Offer not valid in Quebec. Books received may not be as shown. All orders subject to approval. Credit or debit balances in a customer's account(s) may be offset by any other outstanding balance owed by or to the customer. Please allow 4 to 6 weeks for delivery. Offer available while quantities last.

◀ If offer card is missing write to: Reader Service, P.O. Box 1867, Buffalo, NY 14240-1867 or visit www.ReaderService.com ▶

BUSINESS REPLY MAIL
FIRST-CLASS MAIL   PERMIT NO. 717   BUFFALO, NY

POSTAGE WILL BE PAID BY ADDRESSEE

READER SERVICE
PO BOX 1867
BUFFALO NY 14240-9952

NO POSTAGE
NECESSARY
IF MAILED
IN THE
UNITED STATES

No, it didn't, and there was no way to assure Tessa otherwise.

"Dade and I will leave as soon as the night deputies arrive," Grayson said as Dade and he gathered their things. That included backup weapons.

Hell. Landon wanted to go with them. He wanted to help if his cousins were walking into a trap, but he caught a glimpse of something that reminded him of why he should stay put. Or rather a glimpse of someone.

And that someone was Quincy.

The timing sucked. It usually did when it came to Quincy, but this was especially bad. Landon didn't want Quincy to find out Courtney's last known location, since the woman was on the run, probably because of him.

"I need to see you, Deputy Ryland," Quincy said the moment his goon helped him maneuver the wheelchair through the door.

"I don't have time for you right now," Landon fired back. "You need to get out of here."

But Quincy wasn't budging. He had some papers in his hand, and he waved them at Landon. "Here's the proof for me to take my daughter. Now, hand her over to me."

Landon really didn't want to deal with this now, but he was hoping that Quincy's proof was bogus.

"This is the result of the DNA test I had run yesterday," Quincy went on. "I paid top dollars to have the results expedited so I'd know the truth. You lied about the baby being yours, and you'll both pay for that lie. Did you honestly think you could keep my daughter from me?"

That was the plan, and Landon wanted to continue with that plan.

He went to Quincy and took the papers, and Tessa hurried toward them so she could have a look, as well. Grayson and Dade stayed back, watching, but both his cousins knew how this could play out if the test results were real.

And they appeared to be.

Appeared.

Landon handed off the paper to Dade so his cousin could call the lab and verify that a test had been done.

"Where did you get the baby's DNA?" Landon asked.

"From Courtney's place in Austin. There was a pacifier in the crib, and I had it tested."

Landon glanced at Tessa to see if that was possible, and she only lifted her shoulder. So, yeah, it was possible. But Landon had no intentions of giving Quincy an open-arms invitation to take a child he'd fathered. Any fool could father a baby.

"Did you just admit that you broke into your ex's house?" Landon pressed.

Clearly, Quincy didn't like that. He leaned forward and for a moment looked ready to come out of that chair and launch himself at Landon. "You can't keep my daughter from me," Quincy snarled.

Maybe not forever, but he darn sure could for

now. "A DNA test is a far cry from a court order. I'm guessing even with that so-called proof, which can easily be faked, by the way, that you'll have trouble getting custody. Plus, you haven't proven that the DNA from the pacifier even belongs to the baby we have in custody. So leave now and come back when and if you have a court order."

Quincy would have almost certainly argued about that if the two trucks hadn't pulled to a stop in front of the building and the deputies hadn't hurried inside.

"What's going on?" Quincy asked.

Landon didn't answer, but he did motion for the goon to get Quincy moving. "Either you can leave or I'll arrest you both for obstruction of justice." A charge like that wouldn't stick, of course, but at least Quincy would be locked up.

Quincy glanced at all of them, and while it was obvious he thought this was somehow connected to him, he didn't argue. He said something under his breath to the hired goon, and the guy wheeled him out of the sheriff's office.

"This isn't over," Quincy said from over his shoulder. It sounded like the threat that it was.

"He'll try and follow you," Landon reminded Dade and Grayson.

Grayson nodded, and Dade and he headed out the back.

"I'm not giving Quincy the baby," Tessa insisted.

Just lately they hadn't been in complete agreement, but they were now. Landon put his hand on her back to get her moving to Grayson's office, but they'd hardly made it a step when Landon heard a sound of glass shattering behind them.

He turned to step in front of Tessa, but it was already too late.

The blast tore through the building.

ONE SECOND TESSA was standing, and the next she was on the floor. It took her a moment not only to catch her breath but to realize what had happened. Someone had set off some kind of explosive device.

Oh, God.

Just like that, her heart was back in her throat, and her breath was gusting. Someone was trying to kill them. Again.

Cursing, Landon drew his gun, and in the same motion, he crawled over her. Protecting her again. But not only was he putting himself in danger, Tessa wasn't even sure it was possible to protect her. The front door had been blasted open and one of the reinforced windows had broken.

"Car bomb," she heard Landon say, though it was hard to hear much of anything with the sound of the blast still ringing in her ears.

The words had hardly left his mouth when there was a second explosion, and even though Tessa hadn't thought it possible, it was louder than the first.

Landon caught on to her, scrambling toward Grayson's office, and he pushed her inside. But he didn't come in. He stayed in the hall with the gun ready and aimed.

"The deputies?" Tessa managed to say. She wasn't sure where they were, though she could hear them talking.

"They're fine."

Good. That was something at least, but another blast could bring down the building. Plus, they had Grayson and Dade to worry about. They were outside, somewhere, and while they'd gone out through the back, that didn't mean someone hadn't been waiting there to ambush them.

If so, the photo of Courtney had been a trap.

That sickened Tessa, but if that was indeed what it'd been, that didn't mean Courtney had wanted this to happen. Courtney would have likely been forced to have that picture taken. Which meant she was innocent.

"Stay down," Landon warned her when Tessa lifted her head.

She did stay down, but Tessa crawled to the desk, opened the center drawer and found exactly what she'd hoped to find.

A gun.

She wasn't a good shot, but she needed some way to try to defend herself if things escalated. And they did escalate.

"There's a gunman!" Grayson shouted.

Tessa couldn't tell where the sheriff was, but the sound of the gunshot confirmed his warning. And from the sound of it, the gunshot came through into the squad room. It wasn't a single shot, either.

More came.

"Hell, there's more than one gunman," Landon grumbled.

Tessa was about to ask how he knew that, but it soon became crystal clear. Bullets started to smack into the window just above her head. The reinforced glass was stopping them. For now. But whoever was firing those shots was determined to tear through the glass.

But how had the shooter known Landon and she were inside the office?

Maybe their attackers had some kind of thermal scan or were on the roof of one of the nearby buildings. Not exactly a thought to steady her nerves, because it was daylight and any one of those shots could hit an innocent bystander.

"One of them is using an Uzi," Grayson called out. "Everybody stay down."

Tessa certainly did, but Landon didn't. He scurried toward her and maneuvered into the corner so that the desk was between the window and her. Not that it would do much good. The Uzi could fire off a lot of shots in just a few seconds, and it wouldn't be long before those bullets made it through the glass, and then Landon and she would be trapped. He must have realized that, too.

"We have to move," he said. "Stay low and go as fast as you can."

Tessa barely had time to take a breath before Landon had them moving. He stayed in front of her as they barreled out into the hall, and he didn't waste a second shoving her into the interview room where Ward had been just minutes earlier.

She caught a glimpse of the shooter then. One of them, anyway. The man had on a ski mask and was behind a car parked in front of the café across the street. The position gave him a direct line of sight into the sheriff's office, especially now that the door was open. And the shooter made full use of that.

He fired at Landon.

The bullet came too close, smacking into the wall right next to Landon's hand. Tessa latched on to his arm and pulled him into the room with her, and she prayed the deputies were doing something to stay out of the path of those shots. There was another hall leading to the holding cells on that side of the building, so maybe they'd used that.

More shots.

Maybe some of them were coming from Grayson or Dade, though it was hard to tell. Though it wasn't hard to tell when Landon fired. He leaned out the doorway, took aim and pulled the trigger.

"The shooter got through the window," Landon growled.

Mercy. That meant he was in the building, and if this was the gunman with the Uzi, he could mow them all down.

Landon fired another shot. Then another.

It was hard for Tessa to see much of anything, but she did catch a glimpse of a man peering out from Grayson's office. He, too, wore a ski mask and what appeared to be full body armor.

Landon had no choice but to duck back into the interview room when the guy started firing, but there was no way they could let this monster get any closer. Though she knew Landon wasn't going to like it, she lifted her head and body just enough to fire a shot.

She missed.

The bullet tore into the office doorjamb, but it must have distracted the guy just enough. Landon cursed—some of the profanity aimed at her—and he fired again. This time at the guy's head.

Landon didn't miss.

Tessa heard the shooter drop to the floor. Thank God. But she also heard someone else.

The shots stopped.

The relief washed over her. Until Grayson shouted out something she didn't want to hear.

"The second gunman's getting away!"

Chapter Eleven

Landon wanted to kick himself. Two attacks now at the Silver Creek sheriff's office. And either attack could have killed Tessa, his cousins or the other deputies. They'd gotten damn lucky that there hadn't been more damage and there had been no injuries.

Of course, one of the shooters hadn't had much luck today.

The guy was dead, but that wasn't exactly a dose of great news for Landon. Just like the gunwoman from the day before, dead shooters couldn't give them answers, but maybe Grayson and the others would be able to find the gunman who'd gotten away. While Landon was wishing, he added that the moron would cough up a name of who was behind the attacks.

And that they'd find Courtney.

The last might not even be doable. When the deputies had finally made it out to the bridge, there'd been no sign of the woman. If someone was holding her captive, then it was possible that person had taken her far away from Silver Creek.

Tessa got out of the truck and went into the guest-house ahead of Landon. As instructed, she hurried, and that precaution was because of the stranger one of the hands had seen in the area just minutes before the attack at the sheriff's office. Landon doubted that was a coincidence, and because of the possible threat and the attacks, everyone was on high alert.

By the time Landon got inside, Tessa was already at the bassinet and was checking on the baby—who was sleeping. At least Samantha was too young to know what was going on. That was something.

Tessa sighed and touched her fingertips to the baby's hair. She didn't have to tell him that she was worried about both Courtney and the little girl. There were threats all around them, and not all of those threats came from armed thugs. The biggest threat could come from the child's own father.

Landon thanked the nanny and Gage for staying with the baby, but he didn't say anything to Tessa until the two had left. Since he was essentially planning a crime, it was best not to involve his cousin and the nanny.

"If Quincy gets the court order," Landon told her, "we'll take the baby from the ranch. I know a place we can go."

"A safe house?"

"Not an official one. I don't want to go through channels for that, but it'll be a safe place." He hoped. And not just safe. But a place they could stay until they managed to stop Quincy from taking the newborn.

She nodded, and Landon nearly told her to go

ahead and pack. Then he remembered Tessa didn't have much to take with her. It wouldn't take them long at all to get out of there if Quincy showed up with the law on his side.

"Why don't you try to get some rest?" Landon suggested. "You've been through a lot today."

"You've been through worse," Tessa quickly pointed out. "You had to kill a man."

Yeah, a man he would kill a dozen times over if it meant neutralizing the threat. Except there was more to it than that, and even though Landon tried to push it aside, the thought came anyway.

He'd kill to protect Tessa.

Hell.

This was about that blasted attraction again.

"I'm sorry about all of this," she added, and when she turned away from him, Landon knew there were tears in her eyes.

She was coming down from the adrenaline rush, and soon the bone-weary fatigue would take over, but for now there was no fatigue. Just her nerves firing. Landon's nerves were doing some firing, too, but unfortunately, his body was coming up with some bad suggestions as to how to tame those nerves.

"This isn't your fault," Landon said.

They weren't just talking about the danger now. Somewhere in the past couple of seconds, they'd moved on from nerves, danger and gunmen to something so basic and primal that he could feel it more than the nerves.

"I'm sorry about this, too," Tessa whispered, and she went to him, sliding right into his arms.

And Landon didn't stop her. Heck, if she hadn't come to him, he would have gone to her. That meant this stupid mistake was a little easier to make.

Landon hated that she landed in his arms again. Hated it mainly because it was the only place he wanted her to be. Along with giving her some comfort, it was doing the same thing to him. But it was also playing with fire. Having her in his arms made him remember how much he wanted her, and sadly, what he wanted was a whole lot more than a hug.

"Don't," he said when she opened her mouth, no doubt to remind him, and herself, that this was a bad idea.

Since he'd stopped her from putting an end to this, Landon decided to go for broke. He lowered his head, brushed his mouth over hers.

Oh, man.

There it was. That kick of heat. And it wasn't necessarily a good kick, either. It made him go for more than just a mere touch of the lips. If he was going to screw up, he might as well make it a screwup worth making.

He kissed her, hard and long, until he felt her melt against him. Of course, the melting had started before the kiss, so it didn't take much for him to hear that little hitch in her throat. Part pleasure, part surprise. Maybe surprise that they were doing this, but Landon figured it was more than that. Every time he kissed Tessa, he got that same jolt, the one that told him that no one should taste as good as she did.

Especially when she had trouble written all over her.

But it wasn't trouble on her face when she pulled back a fraction and looked up at him. "This can't go anywhere," she said.

The voice of reason. It couldn't go anywhere. He couldn't lose focus, couldn't get involved with someone in his protective custody. Plus, there was that whole thing about not wanting his heart stomped on again.

All of that didn't stop him, though.

Worse, it didn't stop Tessa.

She slipped her hands around him and inched him closer. Of course, the closeness only deepened the kiss, too, and the body-to-body contact soon had them grappling for position. Landon knew what position he wanted—Tessa beneath him in bed. Or on the floor. At the moment, he didn't care.

But the baby had a different notion about that. Samantha squirmed, made a little fussing sound, and that was enough to send Tessa and him flying apart. She turned from him but not before Landon saw the guilt.

Guilt that he felt, too.

He would have mentally cursed himself about it if his phone hadn't buzzed. Maybe this would be good news to offset the idiotic thing he'd just done. No such luck, though. Landon didn't recognize the number on the screen.

While Tessa tended to the baby, Landon answered
the call, but he didn't say anything. He just waited for
the caller to speak first. He didn't have to wait long.

"It's me, Courtney Hager," the woman said. Her
words and breath were rushed together. "Is the baby
okay?"

"She's fine. Safe."

"You have to get a message to Tessa for me,"
she said before Landon could add anything else.
"Please."

"Where are you? Are you all right?"

His quick questions got Tessa's attention, and she
hurried back toward him. However, he also motioned
for her to stay quiet. If someone was listening and
had put Courtney up to this, he didn't want to confirm to that person that Tessa was with him.

"I'm just outside of town," Courtney answered
after several snail-crawling moments, "but I won't be
here much longer. I have to keep moving. If I don't,
they'll find me."

"Tell me where you are, and I'll send a deputy to
get you," Landon insisted.

"You can't. Not now. They know the general area
where I am, and if they see a cop, they'll find me.
Just tell Tessa that I need her to meet me on the playground of the Silver Creek Elementary School. And
don't bring the baby. It's not safe."

You bet it wasn't. "It's not safe for Tessa and you,
either," Landon pointed out.

"I know." A hoarse sob tore from her mouth. "But
I don't have a choice. You can come with Tessa, only

you, but don't bring more cops or else it'll just put us all in even more danger."

"Who'll put us in danger?" Landon pressed.

"I'm not sure, but I need to give Tessa something. Only Tessa. She's the only one I trust. If she doesn't come, I'll have to keep running. Tell her to meet me tonight after dark. And tell her to be careful to make sure she's not followed."

"Where are you right now?" Landon didn't bother to bite back the profanity he added at the end of that.

Another sob. "Please have Tessa come." No sob this time. Courtney gasped. "Oh, God. They found me again."

As much as Tessa wanted to get Courtney out of harm's way, she prayed she wasn't trading her friend's safety for Landon's. Nothing about this felt right, but then it'd been a while since Tessa had felt right about anything. Someone wanted her dead, and that someone might want Courtney dead, too.

And Tessa didn't know why.

But maybe Courtney could help with that.

Courtney had said she wanted to give Tessa something. Evidence maybe? Whatever it was, it could turn out to be critical. Or it could lead to Landon and her being in danger again.

"I really wish you'd reconsider this," Landon repeated to her, and Tessa knew even when he wasn't saying it aloud, he was repeating it in his head.

Landon didn't want her going into town, where they'd already been attacked twice, but like Tessa, he also wanted to find Courtney and get some answers. If they could protect the woman and if Courtney was innocent in all of this, then she could eventually take custody of the baby, and that meant Quincy wouldn't stand much of a chance of getting custody.

She hoped.

Of course, there were a lot of *ifs* in all of this.

Tessa wasn't sure where Courtney had been for the past few days, and it was possible the woman was involved in something criminal. After all, why hadn't she just gone to the cops instead of asking to meet Tessa?

Then there was the matter of the phone Courtney had used to call Landon. When Landon had tried to call her back, she hadn't answered, and it hadn't taken him long to learn that it was a prepaid cell. Of course, it was possible Courtney had lost her own phone. Tessa had. But then whose phone had she used to make that critical call to Landon?

They found me again.

Tessa had heard the terror in Courtney's voice and that wasn't the voice of someone faking her fear. At least, Tessa didn't think it was.

"You trust Courtney?" Landon asked as they drove toward town. He was an uneasy as Tessa was, and both of them looked around to make sure no one was following them.

"I want to trust her," Tessa settled for saying.

It wasn't enough, and that was why Landon had arranged for some security. There was a truck with two ranch hands following them. Two of his cousins, Gage and Josh, had been positioned on the roof of the school building for hours. Added to that, there were two deputies waiting just up the street. If anything went wrong, there'd be five lawmen and two armed ranch hands to help.

But that wouldn't stop another sniper with an Uzi.

Yes, this was a risk, and if Tessa could have thought of another way, she would have done this differently.

Landon had instructed the deputies and the hands to stay back and out of sight. Of course, anyone looking for Courtney would also be looking for any signs of the cops. If the person or Courtney spotted them, it might put a quick end to this meeting, but Tessa had no intention of doing this without backup.

"Remember, when we get there, I don't want you out of the truck," Landon instructed as they approached Main Street. "I'll meet with Courtney, get whatever it is she wants to give you and then talk her into coming back with us so I can put her in protective custody." He paused. "Any other ideas as to what it is Courtney wants to give you?"

They'd already speculated about the obvious—some kind of evidence. Evidence perhaps linked to the attacks. Or maybe even Emmett's murder. After all, Courtney had been at Tessa's place the night Emmett was killed, so maybe Courtney had seen something. Maybe she had even picked up a shell casing or something the killer had left behind.

Tessa had to shake her head, though. If she'd

found something like that, then why hadn't she just gotten it to the cops somehow? Unless…

"Maybe Courtney saw the person who killed Emmett," Tessa speculated. "Or maybe she found out Ward had hired the killer. If she saw Ward's badge, she might believe she can't trust anyone in law enforcement."

Landon made a sound of agreement, but his attention was already on the school just ahead. "If anything goes wrong, I want you to stay down."

Tessa wanted to tell him to do the same thing, but she knew he wouldn't. Landon believed that badge meant he had to do whatever it took to make sure justice was served. Even if this was just another trap.

"Someone could be holding Courtney," Tessa said, talking more to herself than Landon. She remembered the photo of Courtney's bruised face.

"That's my guess, too, but if someone's with her, Gage will let us know. He'll let us know when he spots her, as well."

Since there'd been no calls or texts from any of his cousins or the deputies, Courtney probably hadn't arrived yet. Or else she was hiding and waiting for Tessa to show.

At least there was one silver lining in this. The baby was at the main ranch house with Mason and Grayson. Both would protect the baby with their lives. Tessa just hoped it didn't come down to that.

Landon pulled to a stop next to some playground equipment, and he fired glances all around them. Tessa did the same, but the only thing she saw was the truck with ranch hands parking just up the road from Landon's own vehicle. When they didn't spot Courtney, Landon took out his phone, and Tessa saw him press Gage's number.

"See anything?" he asked Gage.

"Nothing. You're sure she'll show?" Even though the call wasn't on Speaker, Tessa had no trouble hearing him in the small cab of the truck.

"I'm not sure of anything. If she's not here soon, though, I'm taking Tessa back to the ranch."

"Agreed," Gage said, and he ended the call.

Landon hadn't even had time to put his phone away when it buzzed, and he showed her the screen. It was the same number Courtney had used for her earlier call. Landon pushed the button to take the call and put it on Speaker, but he didn't say anything.

"Is the baby safe?" Courtney asked the moment she came on the line.

"Yes. Now, help us to keep it that way."

"I tried. I'm *trying*," she corrected. "I told you to come alone with Tessa," Courtney continued. "There are two cops on the roof. Send them away, and we'll talk."

"We'll talk right now," Landon snapped. "Someone's trying to kill Tessa, and you put her at risk by having her come out here. The cops on the roof are my cousins. They're men I trust, and that's a lot more than I can say for you right now. Tell me why you dragged us out here."

Tessa pulled in her breath, waited. Courtney could

just hang up and disappear. And that was why she had to do something.

"Quincy's trying to take the baby," Tessa blurted out. "He's getting a court order."

"Oh, God," Courtney said, and there was no way that emotion was faked. Tessa could feel the pain. "You can't let him have her."

"Then come out of hiding," Landon insisted. "Let us protect both Samantha and you."

"I can't," Courtney said, and this time Tessa heard more than just the fear. She heard the woman sobbing. "I'd hoped they wouldn't still be on my trail, that I could meet you face-to-face, but I can't. They're following me, and I'd just lead them straight to the baby."

"Who's following you?" Tessa and Landon asked at the same time.

"Gunmen. There are two of them. They caught me by the bridge and forced me to take a picture with a sign that said Help Me. I'm guessing they did that to lure you out to help me, but when they tried to shove me in a car, I managed to get away."

Tessa and Landon exchanged glances. "Why would those men send the picture of you to Joel Mercer?" Landon asked.

The moments crawled by before Courtney said anything else. "Are you sure the men didn't send the photo to Quincy? I figured they'd send it to him, that maybe they were trying to get money from him because Quincy would pay lots of money to find me."

That knot in Tessa's stomach got even tighter. She

didn't like that Courtney had dodged the question about Joel. To the best of Tessa's knowledge, Courtney didn't know Joel. Or at least, Courtney hadn't said anything about knowing Joel, but if she didn't know him, then why hadn't she just come out and said that?

"So you don't think these men work for Quincy?" Tessa pressed. Later she'd work her way back to the subject of Joel, but for now she wanted to get as much information as possible, and she didn't want Courtney clamming up.

"I don't know. But it's possible they used to work for him. They could have gotten greedy and figured they could use me to get him to pay up. But it's not me Quincy wants. It's the baby."

"So he's Samantha's father," Tessa said.

Courtney didn't jump to answer that, either, and she gave another long pause. "How is he getting a court order to get custody? He's a convicted felon."

"He claims he's got DNA proof," Landon explained.

"No. He couldn't have," Courtney insisted. "Where does he claim he got it?"

"He says it's from a pacifier that he took from your house."

"Samantha never used a pacifier, so whatever he's saying about it is a lie. Have the cops already run a DNA test on Samantha?"

"Yeah. We're waiting on the results now. Anything you want to tell us about that?" Landon challenged. Probably because Courtney hadn't confirmed that Quincy was indeed the baby's father. In fact, her friend hadn't confirmed much at all at this point.

That made Tessa glance around again, and she tightened her grip on the gun Landon had given her. She reminded herself that if this was a trap, Gage and Josh would see an approaching gunman. Ditto for seeing Courtney, too, but it was possible the woman wasn't anywhere near the elementary school.

"When you called, you said you wanted to give Tessa something," Landon reminded Courtney.

"I left it underneath the slide on the playground."

Of course it was in the middle of a wide-open space. A space where a shooter could gun them down.

"What is it?" Tessa asked.

"I can't say over the phone in case someone is listening. Just take it and use it to protect my baby."

Tessa hoped there was indeed something to do that, but the only thing that would make it happen was for Courtney to have the evidence needed for them to make an arrest. But if it was that simple, why hadn't she just said what it was?

"We want to protect you, too," Landon said to Courtney. "Tell me where you are, and I can arrange for Samantha and you to be together at a safe house."

Tessa couldn't be sure, but she thought Courtney was crying again. "I can't risk him finding me in a safe house. For now, just protect my little girl. I'll call you again as soon as I can. I have to go."

"Wait," Landon snapped, but he was talking to himself because Courtney had already ended the call.

As Landon had done with her earlier call, he tried

to phone her right back, but she didn't answer. Tessa listened to see if she could hear a ringing phone nearby but there was nothing. Not a sound. Of course, it was possible that Courtney had put that so-called evidence beneath the slide before she even made the original call to them.

Landon called Josh and filled him in on what Courtney had told them. Judging from Landon's tone, he was just as frustrated with what Courtney had said, and hadn't said.

"Josh is wearing body armor," Landon explained once he was off the phone. He's going out there to retrieve what Courtney left, and Gage is going to keep watch from the roof to make sure no one comes in here with guns blazing."

That jangled her nerves again. She hated that Josh had to put himself out there like that, but whoever was behind this wasn't after Josh. They were after Landon and her. And Courtney. Well, they were if Courtney was telling the truth.

"Stay in the truck," Landon told her, and he opened the door.

Tessa caught on to his arm. "It's not a good idea for you to be out in the open."

"I won't be." He got behind his truck door, using it for cover. "But I want to be in a position to give Josh some backup if he needs it. Just stay down."

She did because Tessa didn't want to distract Landon, but she also kept her gun ready. It seemed to take an eternity for Josh to make his way from the roof to the playground, though she figured it was only a few minutes. With each step he took, her heart pounded even harder and her breath raced. Maybe, just maybe, there'd soon be an end to the danger.

Josh was being diligent, too, his gaze firing all around him, and he hurried to the huge slide that was in the center of the playground. She watched him stoop down and pick up what appeared to be a manila envelope. He didn't look inside. Instead he hurried back to the cover of the building.

Time seemed to stop again, and even though she was expecting the call, Tessa gasped when Landon's phone buzzed. Unlike with the other call, she wasn't close enough to hear what Josh said to him.

"Does it have a name on it?" Landon asked. Again, she couldn't hear, but whatever Josh had told him caused Landon's forehead to bunch up. "Go ahead and get in touch with the lab," Landon added. "Then text me the lab's number in case I need to talk to them, too."

Landon got back in the truck in the same motion as he put away his phone. "It's DNA results," he said.

Tessa's mind began to whirl with all sorts of possibilities. "Whose DNA?"

Landon shook his head. "There are file numbers, but the lab should be able to give us a name. It might take a court order, though."

Which meant more hours, or possibly even days, when they didn't have answers. Was the DNA connected to the baby or did this have something to do with Emmett's murder?

Landon started the engine just as his phone

buzzed again, and Tessa was hoping that Josh had found something else in that envelope. But it wasn't Josh. Tessa saw Mason's name on the screen. This time Landon put the call on Speaker.

"We got a problem," Mason said. "Two men just tried to trespass onto the ranch. And Tessa heard something she didn't want to hear from the other end of the line.

Someone fired shots.

Chapter Twelve

Landon cursed, threw the truck into gear and started driving—fast. His first instinct was to head to the ranch, but that would be taking Tessa directly into enemy fire. Instead, he could drop her off at the sheriff's office so he could go and help Mason. Maybe he wouldn't get there too late.

"Are they shooting at the guesthouse?" Landon asked. Beside him, Tessa was trembling, and she had a death grip on the gun.

Mason didn't answer for such a long time that Landon had his own death grip on the steering wheel. "No," Mason finally said. "That was Grayson and Nate who fired, and they weren't anywhere near any of the houses. They shot the intruders. Both men are dead."

Landon figured that was the best possible news he could hear right now. "Are there signs of any other gunmen?"

"Doesn't appear to be, but the ranch hands will patrol the grounds all night to make sure. I'll also give Gage and Josh a call, but it might be a good idea for all of you to stay away from here until we give you the all clear."

Yeah, Landon agreed. The ranch was essentially on lockdown and needed to stay that way. "We'll be at the sheriff's office until we hear from you. Is the baby okay?"

"She's fine, but she peed on me. Went right through the diaper. I'm not sure why that keeps happening to me whenever I'm around kids."

If this had been another cousin, Landon might have thought Mason was saying that to give them some comic relief, but Mason wasn't the comic-relief type.

"Is Courtney alive?" Mason asked.

"For now. But she didn't show up for the meeting. She did leave us something, though. The results of a DNA test. I'll let you know as soon as we know exactly what it is."

Landon ended the call and raced back to the sheriff's office—though the place no longer felt exactly safe. The boarded-up front of the building had something to do with that. The explosion hadn't done any structural damage, but it would be a while before things returned to normal. That included any peace of mind. They weren't going to get that until this snake was captured and put away.

As soon as they were in the building, Landon moved Tessa back to the interview room. No windows in there, unlike Grayson's office, which also had some parts of it boarded up. He waited in the hall, and it didn't take long for Josh to come through the door. However, Landon could tell from his cousin's expression that it wasn't good news.

"The lab wouldn't give you the DNA results," he said to Josh. Tessa stepped into the hall with Landon.

"Bingo," Josh confirmed. "It's a private facility and can't release them. Hell, they can't even tell me who submitted the test or whose DNA it is."

Tessa nodded, let out a long breath and pushed her hair from her face. He hated to see the fear and frustration on her face. Hated even more that those feelings, especially the fear, were warranted.

"Maybe if you tell the lab it's connected to a murder investigation?" Tessa suggested.

"I already tried that," Josh assured her. "They still want the court order. But I'll get started on it right away."

Since this might take a while, Landon had Tessa sit at the interview table, and he brought her back a bottle of water from the break room fridge. It wasn't much, especially considering she'd hardly touched the sandwiches they'd had before leaving for the meeting with Courtney, but he figured Tessa's stomach had to be churning. His certainly was.

"Stating the obvious here, but Courtney's covering up something," Tessa volunteered.

It was obvious. Too bad the answers weren't equally obvious. "Any idea what?"

She took a deep breath first, then a long sip of water. "Keep in mind that I don't know Courtney that well, but she certainly didn't confirm that Quincy was her baby's father."

Landon nodded. "And she was adamant that Quincy couldn't have gotten Samantha's DNA from a pacifier."

Tessa made a sound of agreement. "Granted, I wasn't around the baby much before Courtney left her with me, but I never saw her with a pacifier. So why would Quincy claim something like that?"

Landon could think of a reason. "A shortcut. Maybe Samantha really is his child, but since he can't get a real DNA sample, he created a fake one."

Of course, that would have taken the help of someone who worked in a lab, but considering Quincy was a criminal, he wouldn't have had any trouble paying someone off to help him out.

"Did Courtney ever mention being with Quincy or any other man, for that matter?" Landon asked.

"No." Tessa didn't pause, either. "She just said things weren't good between her and Samantha's father and that she didn't want him to see the baby."

Hearing that gave Landon a bad feeling. If Courtney knew about Landon's connection to Tessa, the woman could have purposely concealed her involvement with Quincy. Or maybe Quincy had been the one to put Courtney up to meeting Tessa.

But why?

What could Quincy have hoped to gain by having his lover get close to Tessa? As sick as Quincy was, maybe he'd planned on trying to seduce Tessa or something so he could sway her into getting revenge against Landon. That was such a long stretch, though, that he didn't even bring it up to Tessa. Besides, Tessa obviously already had too much to worry about.

"Don't say you're sorry again," Landon warned Tessa when she opened her mouth.

Since she immediately closed her mouth, Landon figured he'd pegged that right.

"I've made a mess of your life," she said. Not an apology but it was still too close to being one, so Landon dropped a kiss on her mouth.

She didn't look surprised by the kiss. Which was probably a bad thing. They shouldn't be at the point where he could just give her random kisses and have Tessa look content about it. But that was exactly how she looked—content.

Then she huffed.

No explanation was necessary. The attraction was there, always there. And they didn't even need a little kiss to remind them of it. This time, though, the attraction didn't get to turn into anything more than a heated look and the half kiss. That was because Landon heard someone talking in the squad room. Someone he didn't want to hear talking.

Because it was Ward.

"What did you find?" Landon heard the man ask. Except it wasn't a simple question. It was a demand.

That got Landon moving back into the hall again, and he didn't bother to tell Tessa to stay put. Whatever reason Ward was there, it would no doubt involve her anyway.

"What are you talking about?" Josh asked.

Ward huffed as if the answer were obvious. "What did you find on the playground? And don't bother to lie and say you weren't there, because I had someone watching the sheriff's office, and he followed you."

Josh looked about as uneasy with that as Gage and Landon. Landon went closer, and he made sure it was too close. Since he was a good three inches taller than the man, Landon figured it was time to use his size to do a little intimidating. But even if he hadn't been taller, he would still have been mad enough to spit bullets, and he was about to aim some of that anger at Ward.

"What the hell do you mean, you had someone watching us?" Landon demanded.

Ward's chin came up, but the confidence didn't quite make it to his eyes. "I told him to stay back, not to interfere with your investigation, and he didn't."

No, but what was disconcerting was that no one had noticed this shadow. Of course, since it was probably a federal agent doing the spying, he could have used some long-range surveillance equipment.

Ward pointed to Josh. "He saw him pick up something, and I want to know what it was."

"Trash," Landon said with a straight face. "We don't like litterbugs around here."

If looks could kill, Ward would have blasted Landon straight to the hereafter. "It was something about Tessa, wasn't it? Or the woman you're looking for—Courtney."

Landon just stared at him. "If you're waiting for

me to make some kind of buzzer sound to let you know you've got a right or wrong answer, that's not going to happen. The Silver Creek sheriff's office has jurisdiction over the investigation into the recent attacks, and if we found anything, we don't have to share it with the feds."

"This is my investigation!" Ward didn't shout exactly, but his voice was a couple of notches above normal conversation. This time he pointed at Tessa. "She's working for Joel. Can't you see that?"

Tessa came forward and faced Ward head-on. "I've had a very bad day," she said. No longer shaky, just pissed off. "And I'm tired of you accusing me of working for Joel. I loathe the man and nearly got myself and others killed because I was trying to find evidence to have him arrested."

"I don't believe that," Ward argued.

"Tough." Tessa's index finger landed against his chest. "Because until you have some kind of proof, I want you to stay far away from me and anyone connected to me." She turned to go back toward the interview room.

"I can't do that," Ward said. "Because I need to find Courtney Hager."

That stopped Tessa in her tracks, and she turned around slowly to face him. "Why? How do you even know Courtney?"

The muscles got to working in Ward's jaw. He put his hands on his hips and lowered his head a moment. "I can't tell you. But she's part of a federal investigation."

Mentioning federal was probably a dig at Landon since he'd just played the local-jurisdiction card on Ward.

"A word of advice when it comes to Courtney," Ward continued a moment later. "Don't trust her and don't believe a word she says."

"Why?" Tessa repeated.

But Ward only shook his head. "If you find her, turn her over to me. I'm the only one who can stop her from being killed."

And with that, Ward turned and walked out. Landon didn't bother to follow him and press him for more. They might both have badges, but that was where the similarities ended. They clearly were on opposite sides here, but Landon had to repeat Tessa's *why.*

"If he knows Courtney," Tessa said, "then maybe all of them are connected somehow—Joel, Quincy, Ward and Courtney."

Yeah, but how?

"I'm calling Kade," Landon explained, taking out his phone. "He's still with the FBI, and he might be able to find a link if there is one."

When his cousin didn't answer, Landon left him a message to find out if Courtney was in some witness protection program or was a criminal informant. Those two were the most obvious connections, but when people like Joel and Quincy were involved, it was possible this was a plain and simple criminal operation.

And that Courtney was part of it.

"We can't keep letting this go on," Tessa said. "And I've got an idea how to stop it."

That got not only Landon's attention but his cousins' attention, as well.

"I'm sure it's all over town that I was drugged," she continued. "Everyone probably knows I can't remember all the details of what happened the night Emmett was killed."

"Because someone drugged you," Josh provided.

Tessa nodded. "But what if we spread the word that I am remembering, and the memories are becoming clearer. We could even say I'm planning to go through hypnosis or take some kind of truth serum so I can identify Emmett's killer."

Landon was the first to curse, but Josh and Gage soon joined in, all of them telling her variations of no way in hell was that going to happen.

Landon huffed after he finished cursing. "You would make yourself an even bigger target than you already are."

She lifted her hands, palms up. "Someone wants me dead. I can't imagine that target can get any bigger."

"Well, imagine it," Landon snapped. "This killer will stop at nothing to come after you."

"Apparently, he, or she, will come after me anyway. The killer, the person who hired him or both think I saw something that night. I don't think I did, but hypnosis couldn't hurt. Heck, I might remember exactly what we need to catch this person, and if I don't, the mere threat of me remembering could lure him or her out."

"And you could be killed." Hell. Landon didn't need to say that aloud. Especially since she could be killed with or without the hypnosis, but he wanted to find another way. One that wouldn't put a bull's-eye on Tessa's back.

"You don't want to hear this," Josh said to him, "but Tessa is right. This could work."

"You're right. I don't want to hear it." Landon cursed some more. It didn't help. Because damn it, Josh was right. It could work. Still, Landon couldn't make a call like that.

And that made him stupid.

Because he had done exactly what he'd said he wouldn't do—he'd gotten personally involved with Tessa. He'd lost focus. That could be doubly dangerous for Tessa, the baby and anyone else around them.

Gage went closer, tapped Landon's badge. "You need to be thinking with this right now. We could use the next twelve hours to get everything ready, and this time we could maybe get ahead of an attack."

Hell, Gage was right, too, but that still didn't make this any easier to swallow. Landon was about to do what he didn't want to do. Give in. But before he could do that, his phone buzzed, and he saw Grayson's name on the screen. He got an instant punch of fear because this call could be to tell them that there was another intruder at the ranch.

"What's wrong?" Landon said the moment he answered, and he hoped he was just jumping to conclusions.

He wasn't.

Landon could tell from Grayson's pause. And Tessa must have been able to tell from Landon's expression, because she hurried to him.

"Is it the baby?" she asked.

In case it was, Landon didn't put the call on Speaker. He just waited for Grayson to continue.

"The sheriff over in Sweetwater Springs called," Grayson continued. "They found a body."

"Courtney?" Landon managed to say.

"No. It's a man, and there's no ID yet, but there was a note."

Everything inside Landon went still. Everything except that gut feeling that he was about to hear something he didn't want to hear.

"The sheriff sent me a picture of a note," Grayson explained, "and I'm sending it to you now."

It took but a couple of seconds for Landon's phone to ding, indicating that he had a text, and it took a few more seconds for the photo to load.

Yeah, this was bad. And not bad just because the note was on a dead man's chest. But because the note was addressed to Landon. *This is for you, Landon. Keep protecting Tessa, and there'll be another dead body tomorrow.*

Chapter Thirteen

Tessa didn't regret putting this plan into motion. Especially after seeing the photo of the note that'd been left on a dead man. But it was hard to tamp down all the emotions that went with making herself bait for a killer.

At least the baby was safe. That was something. Before Landon and the other deputies had leaked the news about her impending hypnosis, they'd made arrangements for a safe house and moved Samantha from the ranch. Along with two lawmen and a nanny. Considering there'd been two attempts by intruders, that was a wise thing to do anyway. It got not only Samantha out of immediate danger but also everyone else on the ranch.

Judging from Landon's expression, though, that was the only thing he thought was *wise* about this plan.

But they'd taken other precautions that Tessa felt fell into the wise category. After Grayson and Landon had hashed out the details, they'd agreed that it would be too risky to actually bring in a hypnotist. The killer might try to stop that before the person could even get inside the building. Instead, Grayson had put out the word that the hypnosis session would be done via the computer with an undisclosed therapist.

While Tessa was at the sheriff's office.

That would keep the hospital staff safe, but what it wouldn't do was get Tessa the session that might truly end up helping her recover any lost memories. At least, she wouldn't get the session today. There hadn't been enough time to set that up, but if this trap didn't get them the killer, then that was the backup plan.

"All the reserve deputies are in place," Grayson said when he finished his latest phone call. All of the Ryland lawmen at the sheriff's office—Grayson, Dade, Josh and Landon—had been making lots of phone calls to set all of this up. All doing everything possible to make sure she was safe.

Maybe it would be enough.

"Where are the reserves?" Landon asked.

"Both ends of Main Street, and I've got the other two positioned on the roofs of the diner and the hardware store."

Good. That would stop someone from launching an attack like the previous two. Tessa also knew that security had been beefed up at the ranch just in case the snake after them hadn't gotten the word that the baby had been moved.

"The reserves have orders to stay out of sight," Grayson added. "I've also put out the word that most of the deputies are tied up with the two intruders who were killed at the ranch."

Tessa approved of that, as well. Their attacker might not come after them if he or she sensed this was a trap. Of course, the person had been pretty darn bold with the other attacks, so maybe that wouldn't even matter. Whoever was behind this had no trouble hiring thugs to do their dirty work. That was the reason Landon had insisted on having her wear a bulletproof vest, but she'd put it beneath her shirt in case someone had been watching her go into the sheriff's office.

"We struck out on the dead guy in Sweetwater Springs," Dade said, joining the others and Tessa in the center of the squad room. "He was a homeless guy and doesn't seem to have a connection to any of our suspects."

Which meant he'd been killed just to torture and taunt Landon. And it was working. Every muscle in his body was tight to the point of looking painful, and Tessa figured that wouldn't get better until this was over.

"What time is the hypnosis session supposed to take place?" she asked.

Grayson checked the time. "Right about now. Why don't you go into the interview room and pretend to get started?"

That room had been chosen because there were no windows to guard, and the only way to get in was through the door. A door that Landon was personally guarding.

Tessa sank down at the table to wait. She wasn't certain how long a real hypnosis session would take, but it was possible the killer would try to put a quick end to it. Which meant bullets could start flying at any moment. Or this trap might fail. After all, the killer could just go after her when she finally left the office, but then he or she wouldn't be able to put an end to those possible memories before she could tell anyone else about them.

"You can still back out of this," Landon assured her.

Yes, but everyone in the building knew that wasn't going to happen. Tessa only shook her head. "This could all be over this morning. And then your life can get back to normal."

Of course, it would never be normal for Landon or the rest of his family, because even if they caught Emmett's killer, Emmett would still be dead. It wouldn't even matter why he died, because it would always be such a senseless killing.

She heard the footsteps coming toward the interview room, and Tessa automatically went on alert. But it was just Josh, and he had a very puzzled look on his face.

"Something's going on with the baby's DNA test," Josh said. "I just got off the phone with the lab, and they told me the test results have been suppressed."

"Suppressed?" Tessa and Landon repeated together.

Josh shook his head. "Apparently the feds have removed both the DNA sample and the test results from the lab, and they aren't making them available to anyone else in local law enforcement."

Tessa had no idea what that meant. "Why would they do something like that? And what about the other DNA results Courtney gave us?"

"Those are being released," Josh explained. "Well, partially, and only to us. According to those tests, Quincy isn't the father." He paused. "Emmett is."

That brought Grayson and Dade into the hall with them, and the cousins were as stunned as Tessa was. But it was more than just being stunned. This didn't seem right.

"Emmett and Annie were in love," Tessa said. "Before Annie died, they were trying to start a family. They were happy. I can't believe Emmett would have cheated on his wife, much less gotten Courtney pregnant."

All of the lawmen made sounds of agreement, but she could also feel the doubts. They looked at her as if she might have solid information about this. She didn't. But it did jog something in her head. Something Tessa hadn't remembered until now.

"Courtney and Emmett were talking when she came to my house that night he was killed. I didn't hear what they said, but the conversation was tense. Maybe even an argument."

Landon cursed. "Why didn't you tell us this sooner?" However, he immediately waved that off because he already knew the answer. He'd asked that question only out of frustration. Frustration that

Tessa was certainly feeling, too. "Think hard. Did Courtney ever mention Emmett?"

"No. But Courtney wasn't exactly volunteering anything about her personal life." Which was too bad, because details, any details, would have helped now.

Landon looked at his cousins. "Any idea if Emmett was romantically involved with Courtney?"

Grayson and Dade shook their heads, but Josh shrugged. "You know how Emmett was—not one to spill much about his job or his personal life."

Tessa knew that. It was because as a DEA agent, Emmett often worked undercover assignments that he couldn't discuss, and it was possible that Emmett had wanted some information from Courtney about Quincy.

But she kept going back to Annie.

The one thing Tessa was certain of was that Emmett and Annie had had a good marriage and that he had been torn to pieces when she'd been killed eight months ago in that car crash.

Except…

"What else are you remembering?" Landon pressed.

Landon didn't appear to be fishing with that question, either. He was studying her expression, and that was when Tessa realized her forehead was bunched up.

"It's probably nothing," she said. And hoped that was true. "Annie and Emmett were going through fertility treatments, and Annie was desperate to have a child. Maybe Emmett wasn't as desperate as she was."

No one disagreed with that, and it put a knot in her stomach.

Grayson scrubbed his hand over his face. "Emmett was worried about what the treatments were doing to Annie. But that doesn't mean he would cheat on her. Their marriage was solid."

No one disagreed with that, either. So that meant there had to be some other explanation.

"Maybe the results Courtney gave us are fake," Dade suggested. "Maybe Courtney thinks we'll do more to protect the baby if it's a Ryland."

That could be true, though they were already doing everything humanly possible in that department. "Or maybe Courtney just wanted to make sure Quincy didn't get the baby, and this was her way of making sure of that." Tessa paused. "But that doesn't explain why the feds would suppress the DNA test."

Everyone stayed quiet a moment. "Perhaps the feds aren't suppressing the baby's DNA but rather Courtney's," Landon said.

"Why would they do that?" Though she'd no sooner thrown out that question than she realized why. "You think Courtney is a federal agent or some kind of informant?"

Landon lifted his shoulder. "She could be. If she was a deep-cover operative—a Jane, they call them—then her DNA wouldn't be entered into the system."

True. Because it could get her killed if someone

she was investigating got access to the database and ID'd her as an agent. But Courtney hadn't given her any indications that she was in law enforcement.

And there was something else that didn't make sense.

"If Samantha is Emmett's baby, then why would Quincy believe the child is his?" Of course, Tessa knew the most obvious answer—that Courtney could have been sleeping with both Emmett and Quincy at the same time. No way would she want to tell Quincy that.

The conversation came to a quick halt when Grayson's phone buzzed, and a message popped up on the screen.

"One of the reserve deputies spotted Joel making his way here," Grayson relayed. "He's alone and doesn't appear to be armed."

That didn't mean he wasn't carrying a concealed weapon.

Landon snapped in the direction of the front door. "Hell," he said under his breath.

She certainly hadn't forgotten about Joel, and he was still a prime suspect, but Tessa hadn't expected him to show up. He was more the sort to send hit men to do his dirty work.

"We're busy," Landon snarled. "You'll have to come back."

"Yes, I heard about the busyness going on. Tessa's hypnosis. It's all over town, and I'm guessing you did that to draw out the person trying to kill her."

"Is that why you're here—to try to kill her?" Landon fired back.

"No." Joel stretched that out a few syllables. "I don't want Tessa dead."

She couldn't see his face, but Tessa could almost see the smirk that was surely there. She stood to confront the man herself, but Landon motioned for her to stay put, and he pulled the door nearly shut so there was a crack of only an inch or so. That meant she would still be able to hear the conversation, but Joel wouldn't be able to see that she wasn't going through a hypnosis session.

"Did you miss that part about me saying you'll have to come back?" Landon snapped to Joel.

"No, I didn't, but you'll want me to stay when you see what I've brought you. You wanted proof that Quincy was up to his old tricks. Well, here it is."

Tessa hurried to the door and looked out as Joel handed Landon a piece of paper. She was too far away to see what it was, but it certainly got not only Landon's attention but also his cousins'.

"Where did you get this?" Landon asked.

Joel wagged his finger in a no-no gesture. "I can't reveal my source."

"And that means we can't use this to arrest him." Landon cursed. "Who gave this to you?"

"I meant it when I said I can't reveal my source," Joel insisted. "Because I don't know where it came from. Someone sent it to my office in an unmarked envelope."

Landon glanced back at her to see if she was

watching, and Tessa didn't duck out of the way in time before Joel spotted her.

"Did you remember who killed Emmett?" Joel immediately asked her.

But Tessa didn't answer. She went back into the interview room and kept listening, though she knew Landon would fill her in on what was on that sheet of paper as soon as Joel left. Which would no doubt be soon. No way would Landon want one of their suspects hanging around.

"According to this, Quincy is into gunrunning and drugs," Grayson said, reading through the paper.

"Complete with dates of the transactions and those involved with Quincy," Joel bragged. "I'm not sure exactly who Quincy pissed off, but clearly, the person who sent this is out to get him."

Yes, and it made her wonder why that person hadn't just sent it to the police. Of course, all of this could be some kind of ploy on Joel's part to get the suspicion off him. In fact, Joel could very well be the one behind the gunrunning and drugs, and the names on that paper could be people he wanted to set up to take the fall.

"Say, do you smell smoke?" Joel asked.

Tessa immediately lifted her head and sniffed. She couldn't smell anything, but judging from the way Landon and the others started to scramble around, they did.

Oh, God.

Was this the start of another attack?

Her heart went into overdrive, and even though

she'd tried to prepare herself for this, maybe there was no way to prepare for something like that.

"Get the hell out of here," Landon ordered, and it took her a moment to realize he was talking to Joel.

Joel obeyed, and as soon as he was out the front door, Landon hurried to her.

"Is there really a fire?" she asked, but Tessa soon got the answer, because she smelled the smoke.

"The reserve deputies didn't spot anyone other than Joel near the building," Grayson called out to them. "But there's definitely a fire in the parking lot."

Maybe someone had put some kind of incendiary device on a timer. And maybe it wouldn't stay just a fire once the flames reached a car engine. They could have another explosion.

"Hell," Grayson added a moment later. "There are two fires. Landon and Josh, go ahead and get Tessa out of here. We can't wait around here for the killer to show up."

She reminded herself they'd planned for this just in case they had to evacuate. Landon had parked a bullet-resistant cruiser directly in front of the sheriff's office, and he'd already told her if anything went wrong, he'd be taking her to a safe house. Not the one where they were keeping Samantha but another one so they wouldn't lead the killer straight to the baby.

"Are the reserve deputies sure there are no gunmen in the area?" Landon asked Grayson.

"They don't see anyone."

But that didn't mean someone wasn't out there. Someone hiding in a place the deputies couldn't see.

"You know the drill," Landon told her. "Stay low and move fast."

She did, and Tessa figured she was out in the open only a couple of seconds since she literally stepped right out the sheriff's office and through the back door of the cruiser that Landon had opened for her.

Josh and Landon, though, were outside longer—and therefore in danger—since Landon got behind the wheel and Josh got into the front seat with him. Landon took off right away, but that didn't mean they were safe. In fact, this could be playing right into the killer's hands.

"The reserve deputies will follow us," Josh relayed, and he handed her a gun that he took from the glove compartment. "But they're using an unmarked car."

Good. That meant they'd be close enough to provide backup but without completely scaring off the person responsible for the attacks.

"Where's the killer most likely to come after us?" she asked.

But Landon didn't answer. That was because his head snapped to the left, and Tessa saw the black SUV a split second later.

Before it smashed right into them.

The jolt slammed her against the side of the door so hard that it knocked the breath out of her. Tessa gasped for air all the way, praying that Landon hadn't been hurt or worse. After all, the SUV had slammed into the driver's side. But she couldn't see his arm or shoulder. Couldn't tell if he was bleeding.

"Hold on," Landon shouted, and he gunned the engine.

At least they were able to move and the collision hadn't left them sitting ducks. As soon as Landon sped away, Tessa heard the sound of other tires on the asphalt.

The SUV was in pursuit.

"There's not even a dent in the SUV's bumper," Josh growled, and he turned in the seat to keep watch. He also kept his gun ready, though it wouldn't do any good for him to fire, since the windows on the cruiser would stop his bullet.

That also meant it would stop the bullets of their attackers, but since they must have known that, Tessa figured they had something else in mind.

And they did. The SUV crashed into them again.

This time Tessa went flying into the seats in front of her, and she barely managed to hang on to the gun. Though it was too late, she grappled around and managed to get on her seat belt. Just as the third impact came. She looked behind her and saw that Josh was right—the SUV bumper was still in place, which meant it'd been reinforced.

Landon drove as fast as he could, no doubt trying to get away from Main Street so that no one would be hurt. Plus, they were headed in the direction of one of the reserve deputies though she wasn't sure what he would be able to do. If the bumper on the

SUV had been reinforced, then the windows probably had been, as well.

"Hell," Landon growled.

Tessa looked behind her and saw why he'd cursed. The passenger's-side window of the SUV had lowered, and she saw someone stick out the barrel of a big gun. Except it wasn't just a gun. It was some kind of launcher.

Oh, God.

Were they shooting a grenade at them?

She heard the loud swooshing sound and tried to brace herself for an explosion. But it didn't happen. Instead, something smacked onto the back of the cruiser. Definitely not a grenade. It looked like a lump of clay.

"Get down on the seat!" Landon shouted to her.

Not a second too soon, because they hadn't avoided an explosion after all. The clay must have been some kind of bomb, because the blast tore through the car, shattering the windows and lifting the rear of the cruiser into the air. It smacked back down onto the pavement, stopping them cold.

Tessa hadn't thought her heart could beat any harder, but she was wrong. It felt ready to come out of her chest, but she forced her fear aside because they were about to have to fight for their lives.

The first shot came at them before she could even lift her gun and get it ready to fire. Thank God that Landon didn't have that problem, though. He pushed her down on the seat and fired out the gaping hole in what was left of the back window.

Whoever was attacking them didn't waste any time, either. More shots came, and even though Josh and Landon were using their seats for cover, she knew that bullets could easily go through those.

She didn't dare lift her head, since the SUV was just a few yards from her, but Tessa could see the vehicle in the cruiser's side mirror. And what she saw sent her heart dropping to her knees.

The person in the passenger's seat stuck out that launcher again, and he aimed it right at the cruiser. Sweet heaven. The cruiser wouldn't be able to withstand another direct hit, and that was probably why both Landon and Josh started firing at the guy. He pulled the launcher back inside the SUV. For only a couple of seconds.

Then he took aim at them again.

Tessa prayed this wasn't it, that the three of them wouldn't all die right here, right now. But then she heard a welcome sound.

Shots.

Not ones coming from Josh or Landon. These shots were coming from up the street. Either the reserve deputies had arrived or this was Grayson and Gage coming to help. She hated they were now all in harm's way, but without their help, Landon, Josh and she wouldn't get out of this alive.

She cursed the men trying to kill them. Cursed the fact that she was so close to dying and didn't even know why.

Landon scrambled over the seat, covering her body with his. What he didn't do was fire. Probably because he didn't want to risk hitting his cousins or the other deputies. Josh did fire but that was only when the thug tried to put the launcher out the window again.

The shots outside the cruiser continued, one thick blast after another until they blended together into one deafening roar. But even over the roar, Tessa could still hear another sound.

The squeal of the tires, followed by the stench of the rubber burning against the pavement.

The gunmen were getting away.

Chapter Fourteen

Landon knew they'd gotten darn lucky, but it sure didn't feel like it at the moment.

He'd banged his shoulder when the SUV had first plowed into them, and it was throbbing like a toothache. Josh was limping from a bruised knee. And while Tessa didn't have any physical injuries, she had that look in her eyes that let him know she was on the verge of losing it.

Landon couldn't fault her for that. They'd come so close to dying. Hell, lots of people had since the attack could have turned into a bloodbath on Main Street. However, other than Josh's and his minor injuries, everyone was okay. Again, he qualified that. Everyone was physically okay.

Tessa finished her phone call with the nanny and turned to Landon. "The baby's fine. No sign of any gunmen at the safe house."

That was a relief even though he would have been shocked if attackers had found the location. They'd been careful when they'd moved the baby. Of course, Landon thought he'd been careful with the arrangements he'd made for Tessa, and look how they'd turned out.

Now all he could do was regroup and keep her safe. Not that he'd done a stellar job of that so far, and that meant he had to make some changes. Landon had brought her back to the Silver Creek Ranch guesthouse, but this would be their last night here. In the morning he would put her in Holden's protective custody, and Holden could take her to a real safe house. Then Landon could focus on catching this SOB who kept coming after them.

"Do I need to remind you that the fake-hypnosis plan was my idea?" Tessa said.

She sounded as weary and spent as Landon felt. Maybe even more. He was accustomed to dealing with nightmares like this, but Tessa wasn't. Though lately she'd had way too much experience in that department.

"I'm the one with the badge," Landon reminded her. "I should have done a better job."

"Right, because of those superhero powers you have."

At first he wasn't sure if her smart remark was an insult to point out his shortcomings, but then she lifted her eyebrow. "It was my plan," she repeated. "You got stuck with the mop-up."

"It was more than mop-up," he grumbled. But what he meant to say was that *she* was more than mop-up.

He didn't.

There was already enough dangerous energy

zinging between them without his admitting that he'd been scared spitless at the thought of losing her.

"Besides, I have superhero powers," he added because he thought they could use some levity. "If we ever have to jump a ditch, you'll see what I mean. And I can open medicine bottles on the first try."

She smiled. Which was exactly the response he wanted. But it didn't last. He saw her bottom lip tremble, and just like that the tears watered her eyes. She blinked them back, of course. Landon stayed put, though. That whole dangerous-energy thing was still there.

"I guess you'll be leaving soon," she said, her voice not much louder than a whisper. "Who'll be babysitting me after you leave?"

Landon hadn't said a word to her about the arrangements he'd made shortly after the attack, and he was pretty sure she hadn't heard, because he'd made them when the doctor was checking her. Clearly, Tessa's superhero power was ESP.

"Holden," he admitted. "He'll be here first thing in the morning."

She didn't curse, but some of the weariness vanished, and he was pretty sure she wasn't happy about being traded off to another Ryland. Of course, there couldn't be much about this situation that pleased her, and it was clear he sucked at keeping her out of harm's way.

"You know with me tucked away, it'll be harder for you to catch Emmett's killer," she added.

Hell's bells. He didn't like the sound of that at

all. "You're not thinking about making yourself bait again." And it wasn't a question.

"No. I doubt I could get you or any of your cousins to go along with that. Just reminding you that the killer might just disappear until the dust settles. Or until I come out of hiding." She paused. "Unless you're planning to put me in WITSEC."

Yeah, he was. And since Tessa also hadn't said it as a question, either she truly did have ESP or else she knew him a lot better than Landon wanted her to know him. It was best if he kept some of his feelings from her. Especially the feeling that he was afraid for her, and there weren't many times in his life he'd felt like this.

Tessa scrubbed her hands on the sides of her borrowed dress. "Well, I should probably…do something." She moved as if to go into the kitchen.

And Landon should have let her go. He didn't.

Landon was certain the only thing he didn't want about this were the consequences. And there would be a price to pay, all right. A huge one. Because not only would this make him lose focus, it would take him back to a place he swore he'd never go. A place where he had Tessa in his arms. In his bed.

Knowing all of that didn't stop him from reaching for her.

She was already heading toward him anyway, and it would have been easy to slide right into this without thinking. Landon wanted to think, wanted to remember how he'd felt when she'd walked out on him.

He didn't think, though. Didn't remember.

One touch of his mouth to hers, and there was no turning back. No remembering.

"You don't want to do this," she said, her voice not even a whisper.

"You're wrong." And he proved it.

He slipped his hand around the back of her neck, pulled her against him. Until they were body to body. He'd already crossed a huge line, and there weren't enough superhero powers in the world to make him stop. Tessa seemed to feel the same way, because the moment he deepened the kiss, he felt her surrender. Heck, maybe the surrender had happened even before this. All Landon knew was that this seemed inevitable.

And necessary.

If he'd been given a choice between her and the air he was breathing, he would have chosen Tessa.

Of course, that was the logic of that brainless part of him behind his zipper, but Landon went right along with it. If he was going to screw this up, he might as well make it worth it, even though just being with her seemed to fill the "worth it" bill.

Tessa was still trembling, probably from the adrenaline crash, but Landon upped the trembling by taking the kisses to her neck. Then lower to the tops of her breasts. Even though they had been together but that once, he remembered just how to fire her up.

But Tessa obviously remembered how to do the same to him.

He had her neck at an angle so she couldn't use that clever mouth on him, but she made good use of her hands. First on his chest. She slid her palm all the way to his stomach. And lower.

Definitely playing dirty.

He already had an erection, but that only made him harder. And hotter. To hell with foreplay. If she wanted that, he could give it to her after he burned off some of this fire that she'd started.

Landon enjoyed the sound of surprise, then pleasure, she made when he shoved up her dress and pulled it off her. Now the body-to-body contact was even better because her nearly bare breasts were there for the kissing. Landon fixed the "nearly" part by ridding her of her bra so he could kiss her the way he wanted.

Man, he was in trouble here.

Tessa was the source of that trouble. "I'm not the only one who's getting naked here." And she robbed him of his breath when she shimmied off her panties. "Please tell me you have a condom."

"In my wallet," he managed to say.

Tessa obviously took that as a challenge to get it out, and since Landon was distracted by her naked body, he lost focus long enough for her to go after his wallet. Either she was very bad at that task or else she was doing her own version of foreplay, because by the time she was done, Landon was already lowering her to the sofa.

The moment she had his wallet, she went after his clothes. Landon let her because it gave him a chance to kiss some places he'd missed the first time they'd had sex. It slowed her down a little, and she made a sound of pure pleasure that Landon wished he could bottle. But it still seemed to take only the blink of an eye for her to get off his shirt and boots and get him unzipped.

Landon helped with the jeans and his boxers. Even though this was mindless wild sex, he didn't want anything in between him and her.

And so that was what he got.

He took hold of her, pulling her onto his lap, and in the same motion, he went inside her. Of course, she was familiar, but he still felt that jolt of surprise. Still felt both the relief and the building need. The relief wouldn't last.

The need would.

"We are so in trouble here," she whispered.

Even if he'd had the breath to answer, he wouldn't have argued with her. Because they were. This might be the last time they ever saw each other, and here they were complicating it with sex.

Great sex, at that.

It didn't take long for them to find the right rhythm. Landon caught on to her hips, and Tessa used the rhythm and motion to slide against him.

Yeah, definitely great sex.

He went deeper, faster. Until he could feel Tessa close. That was when he kissed her. It slowed them down a little, but it was worth it. Worth it, too, to watch her as she climaxed. Definitely not a trace of fear or weariness. Only the pleasure.

Tessa gave it right back to him. She kissed him

and gave him exactly what he needed to finish this. Landon gathered her in his arms and let go.

"HELL," LANDON SAID under his breath.

Even though it was barely a whisper, Tessa heard it. She'd figured it would at least be a couple of minutes before Landon started regretting this, but apparently not. *Hell* wasn't exactly the postsex mutterings she wanted to hear.

"Phone," he added.

And that was when Tessa heard the buzzing. A buzzing she'd thought was in her head, but apparently not. Landon moved her off him, frantically dug through the pile of clothes that they'd practically ripped off each other and took his phone from his jeans pocket.

She saw Grayson's name on the screen along with the words Missed Call.

Now it was Tessa who was cursing. This could be something important, a matter of life and death, even.

While he was calling back Grayson, Landon went into the bathroom. She didn't follow him, and he didn't stay in there long. By the time he made it back into the living room, Grayson had already answered.

Tessa hurried to get dressed, and she braced herself to hear that there was another intruder on the grounds. Thankfully, Landon put the call on Speaker, but he probably did that to free up his hands so he could get dressed.

"Everything okay?" Grayson asked.

"Yeah," Landon lied. "What's wrong?"

"Nothing. Well, nothing other than all the other wrong things that have been going on, but we might have gotten a break."

Tessa was so relieved that her legs went a little weak. Of course, that reaction might have had something to do with having a half-naked hot cowboy just a few inches from her. It was wrong to still notice that with the danger all around them, but her body just couldn't forget about Landon.

"That info Joel gave us panned out," Grayson went on. "Though we can't use it as evidence to get Quincy, Dade was able to find a criminal informant who verified that the illegal arms transactions did happen on the dates that were on that paper. Even better, the CI gave us the name of a witness. The transaction happened in San Antonio PD's jurisdiction, so Nate's on his way now to question the witness."

"How credible is this witness?" Landon asked.

"Credible enough. He's a businessman, no record. It appears he didn't know what was going on with the deal and that he got out of it as soon as he realized it was illegal."

It took Tessa a moment to process that, and while it wasn't a guarantee that it would get Quincy out of their lives, it was a start.

"As a minimum," Grayson went on, "this witness can put Quincy in the company of known felons, and that means he can be arrested for a parole violation. If we get lucky, we could have Quincy behind bars tonight, where he'll have to finish out the rest of a twenty-year sentence."

That would mean one of their suspects was off the streets. But Tessa immediately felt the sinking feeling in the pit of her stomach that even that wouldn't help. So far their attacker had only sent thugs after them, and Quincy could still certainly do that from behind bars.

"Is that troubled expression for me or for something else?" Landon asked her the moment he ended the call.

"You and everything else," Tessa admitted. She sank down on the sofa to have "the talk" with him. "What just happened between us doesn't have to mean anything."

He didn't say anything. Landon just waited, as if expecting her to add a *but*. She didn't, because Tessa didn't want him to feel hemmed in, especially since her life was in the air right now.

Landon dropped down on the sofa next to her, took his time putting on his boots and then turned to her. She tried to prepare herself for anything from a thanks to some profanity for what Landon might see as a huge lapse in judgment.

That didn't happen, though.

He kissed her. Not a quick peck of reassurance, either. This was a real kiss. Long and scalding hot. A reminder that what'd just happened did mean something. Well, to her, anyway. It was possible that the kiss was just a leftover response to the attraction.

"Questions?" he asked after he finished that mind-numbing kiss.

Plenty. But she kept them to herself. Good thing, too, because his phone buzzed again. Not Grayson this time. It was Courtney. Landon answered it right away.

"What the hell is going on?" he demanded before Courtney even got a word in.

"I'm sorry," Courtney said after a long pause. "Is Samantha okay?"

"Yes. She's at a safe house. Now, talk."

Courtney didn't do that. Not right away, anyway. "Everything I've done has been to protect my daughter, and I hate that I put you in danger. But I'd do it again if it kept her safe."

"What did you do?" Tessa asked. "And is Emmett really Samantha's father?"

She heard Courtney take a long breath. "I don't want to get into this over the phone. Meet me and we'll talk."

"Talk first and then we'll consider meeting you," Landon countered, and he sounded very much like the lawman that he was. "But I'm not taking Tessa anywhere until I know what's going on, and maybe not even then. You know someone tried to kill her again?"

"Yes, I know. And I'm sorry. So sorry."

"I'm not looking for apologies," Landon snapped. "Answers. *Now*."

Courtney took another deep breath. "I'm a Justice Department operative." And that was all she said for several long moments. "But you might have already guessed that."

"It was one of the theories. I figured that might be why you had Samantha's DNA results suppressed."

"It was. Partly," Courtney added. "And I also had them suppressed because the DNA sample you took from Samantha will prove that Quincy is her father."

Landon didn't say anything, but Tessa could see the relief Landon was feeling because this meant Emmett hadn't cheated on his wife. But she could also see the confusion.

"Right before Emmett was killed," Courtney went on, "he agreed that he would say Samantha was his so that Quincy couldn't get her."

That sounded like something Emmett would do, and that might have been what Emmett and Courtney had been discussing when she'd seen them together.

"You knew Emmett well?" Landon asked.

"Yes. We'd worked together on some investigations. I'm so sorry he's dead."

They all were. But Tessa hoped Courtney could give them some answers. "Do you know who killed him?"

"No," Courtney quickly answered, "and if I did, I would be figuring out a way to make sure his killer gets some payback."

Hard to do that with killers on their trails. "How the heck did you ever get involved with Quincy?"

"I was on a deep-cover assignment, and he helped me make some contacts. Ward introduced us."

That was not a connection that Tessa wanted to hear. "Ward knows you're an agent?" Tessa asked.

"No." Courtney groaned. "Maybe. But he's not supposed to know. I was posing as a criminal informant when I met him. I'm a Jane operative, and there aren't any records about me in any of the regular Justice Department databases, but it's possible Ward hacked into the classified files and found out my real identity. Maybe that's why all of this happened."

"What *did* happen?" Landon pressed.

Again, Courtney paused. "A little over nine months ago, Quincy arranged a meeting with me, and he drugged me. Rohypnol, I think. I blacked out, and when I woke up, I was naked and in bed with him."

Landon cursed, and Tessa couldn't quite choke back the gasp that leaped from her throat. Courtney had been sexually assaulted.

"I would have killed Quincy on the spot, but his thugs came in. At that time he was paying some motorcycle gang to play bodyguard and do his muscle work for him. So I left to regroup, to figure out a way to bring him down. And then I found out I was pregnant."

"You're sure the baby is Quincy's?" Tessa said, though it was a question she hated to ask.

"I'm sure. I had a real DNA test done, but those test results have been destroyed. Emmett was helping with that, and that's why I saw him the night he was killed. He's the one who had those fake results created."

Landon jumped right on that. "You think that's

why Emmett was killed, because he was helping you?"

"I hope not." The sound Courtney made was part moan, part groan. "But I don't know for sure. Quincy could have found out Emmett was helping me and sent this hired muscle after him. I can't rule out Joel, either, because Emmett was investigating him. Both Joel and Quincy certainly have the resources to hire guns not only to kill Emmett but to go after you."

"And Ward?" Landon asked. "Can you rule him out?"

"No," Courtney said without hesitation. "I don't have anything on him, though. I don't have anything to bring anyone to justice. That has to change. I have to make sure Samantha is safe. That's why I gave you those fake DNA results—to protect my baby. I knew Emmett would have done the same thing if he'd been alive."

"He would have," Landon assured her. "But why leave the fake DNA results on the playground like you did?"

"I was hoping Quincy would get word of it. After the fact," she quickly added. "I certainly didn't want him showing up on that playground. I also thought if you believed Samantha was a Ryland, that you'd do everything within and even beyond the law to protect her."

"That was a given," Landon assured her. "She doesn't need Ryland blood for us to do that."

Tessa made a sound of agreement. They were a family married to the badge, and they wouldn't have let a snake like Quincy take the baby. She'd learned that firsthand, but then, Courtney probably felt she needed some insurance with those altered DNA results.

"What do you know about the body that turned up in Sweetwater Springs?" Landon asked. "It had a note similar to the one left on Emmett's body."

"I have no idea." And it sounded as if Courtney was telling the truth. "But that goes back to Quincy, doesn't it? I mean, he's the one with a personal vendetta against you."

Yes, but either Ward or Joel could have used that to set up Quincy. Of course, after what Courtney had just told them about Quincy sexually assaulting her, Tessa wanted the man to pay and pay hard. But she also wanted the same for the person behind the attacks. That way they could get double justice if that person turned out to be Quincy.

"We don't have anything to help with pinning this on Ward or Joel," Landon explained, "but we might have something on Quincy. There's a witness who could possibly help us nab Quincy on a parole violation."

"That won't help. He'll still send someone after Samantha."

Neither Landon nor Tessa could argue with that.

"I'm still weak from the delivery," Courtney added. "That's why I've had such a hard time keeping out of the path of these thugs."

"If you're weak, that's even more reason to let me help you," Landon insisted.

"I do need your help," Courtney agreed. "I have a plan to draw out Quincy. A plan that will put him behind bars for the rest of his life. I'll text you the details. And, Landon, please come. I'm begging you to help me."

Chapter Fifteen

As plans went, there was nothing about this one that Landon liked. Because it stood a good chance of getting Courtney killed. It was also a plan he couldn't stop, since Courtney had already set things in motion.

And that *motion* involved Landon.

"Let me get this straight," Grayson said, sounding as skeptical as Landon and Tessa were, and Landon had no trouble hearing every drop of that skepticism from the other end of the phone line. "Courtney wants you to pretend to bring her baby to the playground at the elementary school so that Quincy's hired guns will believe that she now has the child?"

That was it in a nutshell, and it would put a huge target on Courtney. "She said that Quincy knows Tessa and I have the child, so it'll make it more believable if I show up. Of course, it won't be the real baby. Courtney suggested a doll wrapped in a blanket."

Grayson cursed a blue streak—which had been

Landon's first reaction, as well. "And then what? Quincy's men gun her down and take the 'child'?"

This wasn't going to sound any better than the first part of the plan. "Courtney believes they won't shoot her, because they won't risk hurting the baby." Maybe that would happen. After all, Quincy seemed determined to get his hands on his daughter.

"Then what?" Grayson snarled.

"Then she can use the child to draw out Quincy. When he tries to kill her and take the baby, then she can arrest him for conspiracy to commit murder, rape and other assorted felonies."

Grayson stayed quiet a moment, obviously processing that. "How much time do you have?"

"Not much. Courtney said she'll be at the playground in about thirty minutes from now. If I'm not there with the fake baby, then she said she'll just try to deal with the hired guns to draw Quincy out, that one way or another she's putting an end to this tonight."

More profanity. "And how does she know the hired guns will even be there?"

"Because they've been following her, and she's barely managed to escape them several times." Obviously, once they'd managed to capture her, because that was when the photo of her had been taken. "She said if she steps out into the open, the gunmen will be on to her right away."

"Call her back. Stop this plan," Grayson insisted.

"Already tried. Multiple times. She's not answering her phone."

Courtney probably didn't want Landon trying to talk her out of this, and part of him couldn't blame her. She was a desperate mother trying to protect her baby, but Courtney was taking a huge risk that might not pay off.

"Where are Tessa and you now?" Grayson asked.

"On the way to the sheriff's office. I wanted to leave Tessa behind, but—"

"If this is a trap, I don't want to have gunmen come to the ranch," Tessa interrupted. It was an argument Landon had had with her from the moment they'd read the text with Courtney's plan.

Grayson clearly wasn't pleased about that, either. Welcome to the club. If there was a pecking order for displeasure here, Landon was at the top of it. Taking Tessa out in the open like this was dangerous.

"You're coming here to the sheriff's office?" Grayson asked.

"Yeah." Though that was a huge risk, too, considering everything that'd happened there in the past couple of days. "I have two armed ranch hands and Kade following me into town. I thought it best if the others stayed at the ranch. Just in case."

Though the ranch would probably be the safest place in the county since Tessa, he and the baby wouldn't be there.

"The two night deputies are here," Grayson explained. "Tessa can stay here with Kade and them. I'll go with you and the ranch hands to drop off the doll. I just wish I had more time to bring in backup."

So did Landon, but since Courtney wouldn't even

answer her phone, there was no chance of putting a stop to this meeting. "I'll see you in ten minutes." Well, he would unless they encountered gunmen along the way.

"Stay low in the seat," Landon instructed Tessa. This was a farm road, no streetlights and only the spare lights from the ranches that dotted the area. It would be the perfect place for an attack.

"You think this will fool Quincy's men?" she asked.

She was looking down at Kimmie's doll, which they'd wrapped in a pink blanket. Landon was thankful it had been at the guesthouse or they would have had to go looking for one. When the little girl had brought over the gift for Samantha, Landon hadn't known it would come in so handy.

"It's dark," Landon answered. "And I'll make sure the blanket covers the doll's face."

It was a little precaution, but he'd taken a few bigger ones, too. Like Tessa and him both wearing Kevlar vests. And asking Kade and the ranch hands for backup. Landon had asked them simply because they'd been outside the guesthouse at the time. Patrolling. Right now every minute mattered.

"If shots are fired," Tessa said the moment he made the final turn for Silver Creek, "swear to me that you'll get down."

"They won't fire shots. Not as long as they think I have the baby."

"Swear it," she repeated.

Landon figured the little white lie he was about to tell might steady her nerves. "I'll get down."

And that was partly true. He would indeed get down if he could, but it was a playground. Not exactly a lot of places to take cover. And then there was Courtney to consider. He couldn't just leave her out in the open to be gunned down.

He saw the lights from Main Street just ahead and knew they had only a couple of minutes before he had to drop her off. "If this doesn't work," he added, "you're going into WITSEC first thing in the morning."

Tonight if he could arrange it.

But even that was a lie. Because either way, she'd have to leave. Catching Quincy wouldn't put an end to the danger if it was Joel or Ward who was after them. However, it could get Courtney and the baby out of harm's way.

"So this is goodbye," she said, though judging from the slight huff she made, Tessa hadn't intended to say that aloud.

Landon considered another white lie, but after everything that had happened between them, he couldn't do that to Tessa. "Yes. More or less, anyway. If we get Quincy, I'll be tied up with that, and Grayson can finish up the WITSEC arrangements."

She nodded and glanced at him as if she wanted to say more. She didn't. Not for several long moments, anyway.

"I'm in love with you," Tessa blurted out, and

that time she looked as if that was exactly what she wanted to say.

Hell.

Landon sure as heck hadn't seen that coming.

"I don't expect you to feel the same way," Tessa added, "and I don't expect you to do anything about it."

But she probably did expect him to give her some kind of response, and he would have done just that—even though he didn't have a clue what to say.

But something caught his eye.

They were still several blocks from the sheriff's office, on a stretch of Main Street with buildings and businesses on each side, but he saw the woman.

Courtney.

Landon got just a glimpse of her before she darted into an alley. But he got more than a glimpse of the two men who were running after her. One of those men lifted his gun, aimed it at Courtney.

And he fired.

"GET DOWN!" LANDON SHOUTED to Tessa.

He pushed her lower to the seat, but she was headed in that direction anyway. She also threw open the glove compartment and took out a gun. But before Tessa could even get the gun ready to fire, another shot rang out.

The bullet slammed into the windshield of Landon's truck.

So much for their theory that these goons wouldn't fire because they wouldn't want to risk hitting the baby. If Samantha had been in the truck with them, she could have already been hurt. Or worse.

That gave Tessa a jolt of anger. Not that she needed the thought of that to do it, but it helped. She was fed up with someone putting Landon and the others in danger. Fed up with all these attempts to kill her. She wanted to shout out, demanding answers, but the gunmen obviously didn't have answers on their minds.

They fired more shots into the truck.

"Hold on," Landon said. "I'm getting us out of here."

He threw the truck into Reverse, hit the accelerator and just as quickly had to slam on the brakes. He cursed, and it took her a moment to realize why. The truck with Kade and the two ranch hands was behind them.

But so were two more gunmen.

There was one on each side of the street, and they were shooting into Kade's truck. While in Reverse, as well, Kade screeched out of there, getting out of the path of those bullets, but Tessa figured he would double back to help them.

"Text Grayson." Landon tossed her his phone. "He needs to stay the hell back for now. I don't want him hit with friendly fire."

Neither did she, and while she did the text, she got a dose of what could be friendly fire. Landon leaned out from his truck window and fired at the guys behind them.

That was like turning on a switch. Suddenly,

shots started slamming into the truck, and they were trapped with gunmen both in front of and behind them. Landon put the truck back in gear, jerked the steering wheel to the right and drove into one of the alleys.

But it was a dead end.

"Come on," Landon told her. He took his phone and shoved it in his pocket. "Move fast."

She did. Tessa hurried out of the truck, but she had no idea where they were going. She knew all the shops on Main Street, but she certainly didn't know the back alleys. Thankfully, Landon did. With his left hand gripping her wrist, they ran toward a Dumpster, and he yanked her behind it.

Just as the next shot came.

This one smacked into the Dumpster, the bullet pinging off the metal, which acted like a shield for them. But it wouldn't be a shield for long if all four of those thugs came in there with guns blazing. For now the four stayed back, using the fronts of the buildings for cover.

"Shoot them if they try to come closer," Landon told her, and he began to kick at a wooden fence on the left side of the Dumpster.

Tessa kept watch and tried to tamp down her breathing. Hard to do, though, because she felt ready to hyperventilate. It didn't help when one of the men darted out. She fired.

Missed.

And she fired again.

She wasn't sure if she winged him or not, but at least it got him scurrying back behind the building.

Landon gave the fence a few more kicks, and it gave way. Tessa had no idea what was on the other side, but it was behind the secondhand store run by a local charity group. The area wasn't very wide but was littered with all sorts of discarded furniture and another Dumpster. That was where Landon took her.

There wasn't much light at the back of the building. The only illumination came from Main Street and a pale moon, and there were enough shadows that it would be easy for a gunman to be right on them before she saw him.

"Keep watch there." He tipped his head to the alley between the store and a hair salon. The alley where she'd seen Courtney running. But there was no sign of her now.

What had gone wrong?

Had Quincy realized this was a trick and sent his thugs after her? Probably. This plan had been so risky right from the start, and now Courtney was running for her life again. But then, so were Landon and she.

While he kept watch of the area they'd just left, he also texted Grayson. No doubt to let him know their location. The moment he did that, though, he eased his phone into his pocket and put his finger to his mouth in a "stay quiet" gesture.

And Tessa soon knew why.

She heard the footsteps, and they were coming from both sides of the thrift store. Either the four gunmen had separated and were now in pairs or else this was someone else.

Tessa pulled in her breath. Held it. Waiting.

Other than the footsteps, everything was so quiet. At least for a couple of heart-stopping seconds.

"Ryland?" someone called out. She didn't recognize the person's voice, but it was likely one of Quincy's hired guns. Or whoever's hired guns they were. "Do the smart thing and give us the kid. That's all we want."

So definitely Quincy's men.

Well, maybe.

Unless this was yet another attempt to set him up.

"The kid's not in your truck," the guy continued. "We checked. So tell us where you have her stashed and you and your kin won't die."

Maybe it was out of frustration or maybe just to let the jerk know he wasn't cooperating, but Landon fired a shot in the direction of the voice.

The man cursed, calling Landon some vile names.

"It's me you want," someone else shouted.

Courtney.

Tessa couldn't tell where exactly she was, but she was close. Maybe just one building over.

Now Landon cursed. "Stay down!" he yelled to Courtney.

"No. I'm not going to let Tessa and you die for me. Just promise me you'll take care of my baby."

And then it was as if the world exploded.

The blast came like a fireball to their right. In the same area where Courtney had just been. It was deafening, and the flurry of shots that followed it didn't help. Tessa couldn't tell where the gunmen were, but she had no trouble figuring out where they were aiming all those shots.

At Courtney.

"Don't get up," Landon told her.

But that was exactly what he did. He leaned out from the Dumpster and fired two shots. Even over the din of the other bullets, Tessa could hear that the last one he fired sounded different.

"I got one of them," Landon snarled.

Tessa hated that he'd been forced to kill a man, but she wished he could do that to all four of them.

The fact that one of their comrades had fallen didn't stop the other three from firing. And running. They were heading away from Landon and her and were almost certainly in pursuit of Courtney.

"Stay behind me," Landon instructed. "I need to get you to Grayson so I can help Courtney."

Tessa wanted that. Well, she wanted part of it, anyway. She wanted Landon to save Courtney, but Tessa wasn't certain she'd be any safer with Grayson than she was with Landon.

Landon got them moving again. This time toward the back of the hair salon. It was also the direction of the sheriff's office. Of course, that was still buildings away. To Tessa, it suddenly felt like miles and miles, and it didn't help that the shots were still ringing out.

And getting closer.

God, were those men coming back?

Part of her hoped that meant they'd given up on

chasing Courtney, but her mind went to a much worse scenario. They could have already killed Courtney and were now doubling back to take care of the other lawmen, Landon and her. Since Kade, Grayson and heaven knew who else were out here, the thugs could be firing those shots at them.

There was no Dumpster at the back of the salon, so Landon pulled her into the recessed exit at the rear of the building. It wasn't very deep, just enough for them to fit side by side, and like before, Landon instructed her to keep watch. She did, and Tessa listened.

The shots had stopped, and she could no longer hear footsteps. In fact, she couldn't hear anything, and that caused her heartbeat to race even more. Something was wrong.

And she soon realized what.

The door behind them flew open, and someone put a gun to Landon's head.

"Move and you die," the man growled.

IF IT WOULD have helped, Landon would have cursed, but it wouldn't have done any good. One of the thugs had a gun pointed at him, and that meant Landon had to do something fast before the thug killed him and then turned that gun on Tessa.

"Drop your guns," the man ordered. "Do it!" he added, and this time he put the gun against Tessa's head.

Landon couldn't risk it, so he did drop his gun, but he didn't drop it far. Just by his feet. Tessa did the same, and hopefully, that meant he could grab them if it came down to it. Of course, in the small space, Landon might be able to overpower the guy.

"Who hired you?" Landon asked.

Though he figured getting an answer, much less a truthful one, would be next to impossible. Still, he had to try while he also came up with a plan to get Tessa out of there.

The guy didn't say a word, but Landon could hear some chattering. Probably from a communications earpiece he was wearing. Landon wished he could hear the voice well enough to figure out who was giving these orders.

Landon's phone buzzed in his pocket. Likely Grayson. But he didn't dare reach for it. Grayson would take his silence as a sign he needed help.

"There's no reason for you to keep Tessa," Landon tried again.

"Shut up," the man barked. Judging from the earpiece chatter, he was still getting his orders.

Landon looked at Tessa. He expected for her to be terrified, and she probably was, but that wasn't a look of terror in her eyes. It was determination.

And something else.

She didn't move an inch, but Tessa angled her eyes to the left. It was Landon's blind side because of where he was in the recessed doorway, but Tessa must have seen something. Grayson maybe? Then, she lowered her eyes to the ground for a second.

Landon hoped like the devil that he was making the right interpretation of what she was trying

to tell him—to get down—and he readied himself
to respond.

But nothing happened.

The moments just crawled by with the thug behind
him getting an earful from his equally thuggy boss.
And with Tessa and him waiting. Landon didn't want
to wait much longer, though, because there were two
other hired guns out there somewhere, and he didn't
want them joining their buddy who had a gun on
Tessa.

"Now!" Tessa finally said. She didn't shout it, but
she caught hold of Landon's arms and dragged him
to the ground with her.

Just as the shot blasted through the air.

Even though he'd been expecting something to
happen, his heart jumped to his throat, and for one
sickening split second, he thought maybe Tessa had
been hit. But she wasn't the one who took the bullet.

It was thug number two behind them.

Both the thug and his gun clattered to the ground,
and Landon didn't waste any time gathering up their
weapons and getting Tessa the heck out of there.
Since he figured it was an ally who'd killed the guy,
he followed the direction of the shot, and he got just
a glimpse of Courtney as she ran away. She was the
one who'd fired the shot.

But now someone was firing at her.

The bullets blasted into the walls of the building
as she disappeared around the corner. Landon needed
to disappear, too, or at least move Tessa out of what
was to become a line of fire. It didn't take long for

that to happen. The shots came, and Landon pulled her between the hair salon and the barbershop.

It was darker here than in the back and other side alleys. That was because the perky yellow window awnings on the side of the salon were blocking out the moonlight. Landon could barely see his hand in front of his face, and that definitely wasn't a good thing. He didn't want to run into one of the two remaining gunmen.

Of course, there could be more.

Since that wasn't exactly a comforting thought, he pushed it aside and pulled Tessa into a recessed side exit of the barbershop. They couldn't stay there long, but it would give him a chance to check in with Grayson.

"See who texted me," Landon said, handing Tessa his phone and her gun. Since he didn't want anyone crashing through the door as the other thug had done, he volleyed glances all around him. And listened for footsteps.

"Grayson," she verified. "He wants us to try to get to the bakery shop just up the street. He says we should go inside because the other deputies and he are creating a net around the area. They're closing in to find the gunmen, and they don't want us caught in cross fire."

Landon didn't want that, either, but the bakery had been closed for months now and was probably locked up tight. It was also three buildings away from the barbershop. Not very far distance-wise, but each step could be their last.

"What should I text Grayson?" she asked.

Her voice was shaking. So was she. But then, she'd just had a man gunned down inches behind her. Thank God Courtney was a good shot or things could have gone a lot worse. Though Landon hated that Courtney was having to fight a battle when she'd given birth only a week earlier. It didn't matter that Courtney was a federal agent; her body couldn't be ready for this.

"Give Grayson our location and tell him we're on our way to the bakery." Landon hoped they were, anyway.

It was too risky to head to the street. The lighting would be better there, but it would also make it too easy for the thugs to spot them. Instead, he led Tessa to the back of the building again, and he stopped at the corner to look around.

Nothing.

Well, nothing that he could see, anyway.

He doubted Courtney was still around to take someone out for him, and that meant he had to be vigilant even though he couldn't see squat. However, he could hear. Mainly Tessa's breathing. It was way too fast, and Landon touched her arm, hoping it would give her a little reassurance. It was the best he could do under the circumstances because he had to keep her moving.

Landon dragged in a deep breath, hooked his arm around Tessa's waist and hurried out from the cover of the building. No shots, but Landon knew that could change at any second. As soon as he reached the other side of the barbershop, he stopped again and made sure there wasn't anyone in the alley ready to ambush them.

He cursed the darkness and the shadows, and he moved himself in front of Tessa, racing across the open space to the next building. Two more and they'd be at the bakery. Landon only hoped by the time they made it there, Grayson would have it secured.

"Let's move," Landon whispered to her, and they started across the back of the next building. But they didn't get far before Tessa stumbled.

Landon tightened his grip on her to try to keep her from falling, but she tumbled to the ground anyway. Then he darn near tripped, as well. That was because there was something on the ground. And Landon immediately got a sickening feeling in the pit of his stomach.

Because that something was a dead body.

Chapter Sixteen

Tessa barely managed to choke back the scream in time. A scream would have given away their position, but it was hard not to react when she fell onto the body.

The person was still warm. And there was blood. But Tessa had no doubt that the person was dead, because there was no movement whatsoever.

"Courtney," she whispered on a gasp.

"No, it's not," Landon assured her. But he did more than give her a reassurance. He got her back to her feet and moved her into the alley on the side of a building. Probably because the person who'd done this was still close by.

The light was so dim in this part of the alley that it took Tessa several heart-racing moments to realize Landon was right. It wasn't Courtney. It was a man.

Quincy.

His wheelchair was only a few feet from his body and had been toppled over. There was also a gun near his hand.

What had happened here?

Tessa could think of a couple of possibilities. Maybe he'd been shot in cross fire by the thugs he'd hired? Or maybe the thugs worked for someone else? It was also possible Courtney had done this. After all, Quincy was a threat to the baby, her and maybe anyone else who crossed his path.

It was hard to mourn the death of a snake like Quincy, but Tessa realized the goons were still around because she heard several more shots. If they did indeed work for Quincy, maybe they didn't know their boss was dead.

"We need to keep moving," Landon told her under his breath.

They did, and Tessa forced herself to start running. Landon helped with that again. He took hold of her, and they ran through the back of the alley to the next building. They were close now to the old bakery where Grayson wanted them to go, but it still seemed miles away.

More shots came.

And these were close. Too close. One of them smacked into the wood fence that divided the alley from the town's park, and the shot had come from the area near Quincy's body.

Tessa hoped that once the thugs saw that Quincy was dead, they'd back off, that no more bullets would be fired. But almost immediately, another shot rang out. Then another.

Landon slipped his arm around her, but it wasn't preparation to get them running again. He pulled her deeper in the alley, and his gaze fired all around

them. He stepped in front of her when they heard
some movement near Quincy's body, and Tessa got
just a glimpse of not one of the gunmen but Courtney.

The woman was leaning over Quincy and touched
her fingers to his neck. It seemed as if she was making sure he was dead.

"Courtney," Landon whispered.

Tessa glanced out again and saw Courtney's head
whip in their direction. She got to a standing position and turned, heading their way.

Just as there was another shot.

This one smacked right into Courtney's chest, and
Tessa heard her friend gasp in pain as she dropped
to the ground.

Oh, God.

Courtney had been hit.

The new wave of adrenaline slammed into Tessa,
and she would have bolted out to help her if Landon
hadn't stopped her. Landon cursed and stepped out
from the building, but he almost certainly couldn't
see the shooter, since the bullet had been fired from
the alley of the building over from them.

Courtney groaned, the sound of sheer pain, and
while she was gasping for breath, she was also trying to lift her gun. No doubt trying to stop the gunman before he put another bullet in her.

"She's wearing Kevlar," Landon said.

Because her instincts were screaming for her to
help Courtney, it took Tessa a moment to process
that. The bullet had hit the Kevlar, not her, and that

meant she might not die. Not from that shot, at least, but the next one went into the ground right next to her. The only reason it didn't hit her was that Courtney managed to roll to the side. But Courtney was still writhing in pain, still gasping for air and clearly couldn't get to her feet to run.

Landon's phone buzzed, and Tessa saw Grayson's name on the screen. He passed it back to her so she could answer it.

"What's your position?" Grayson asked.

"We're still two buildings away from the bakery. We need help. Can you get to us?"

"Not right now. We're pinned down. There's a sniper on one of the roofs, and every time we move, he fires a shot. He hit one of the reserve deputies."

That didn't help steady her heart. "Courtney's been hit, too."

Grayson belted out some profanity. "We'll get there as soon as we can." And he ended the call.

Tessa knew that he would, but soon might not be soon enough. Plus, there was no way an ambulance could get anywhere near the scene. Not with all the gunfire.

"I've got to help Courtney," Landon whispered, but Tessa heard the hesitation in his voice. He made a split-second glance at her as she slipped his phone back into his pocket. "Stay put and keep watch around you."

That was the only warning Tessa got before Landon stepped out. He pivoted in the direction of the shooter, and he fired. Tessa prayed that would put an end to the immediate threat.

It didn't.

She saw the gunman's hand snake out, but this time he didn't fire at Courtney. He fired at Landon. Her heart nearly went out of her chest as Landon scrambled to the ground, using a pair of trash cans for cover.

As Landon had told her, she kept watch around her, but Tessa also tried to do something to stop that thug from gunning down both Courtney and Landon. Courtney was in the open, an easy target, and bullets could go through the trash cans where Landon had ducked down. She had to help. She couldn't just stand there and watch them die.

She waited, watching, and when she saw the gunman's hand come out again, she took aim and fired. Almost immediately, the guy howled in pain, and while she certainly hadn't killed him, at least she'd managed to injure his shooting hand. However, that didn't stop him from firing.

Again and again.

The man was cursing, and he was making grunting sounds of someone in pain, but that didn't stop him from pulling the trigger, and he was shooting at Landon. Maybe because he thought Landon had been the one to fire that shot at him.

Courtney moved again, managing to get on her side. And she even tried to take aim, but she was clearly in too much pain to defend herself. The gunman's next bullet slammed into her again, and Tessa heard Courtney's gasping sound of pain.

Mercy, she'd been shot, and this time Tessa didn't think the bullet had gone into the Kevlar. Landon must not have thought so, either, because he came from behind the trash cans and he raced out. Not toward Courtney.

But toward the alley where the gunman was getting ready to send another shot right into Courtney. To finish her off, no doubt.

Landon put a stop to that.

He pulled up, pivoted and double-tapped the trigger.

Even though there had been so many shots fired all around them, those two sent Tessa's heart into overdrive. Because now both Landon and Courtney were in the open, and if Landon's two shots didn't work, then the gunman would try to kill them both again.

Tessa was ready to do something to make sure that didn't happen when she heard the movement behind her. She started to whirl around, bringing up her weapon in the same motion, but it was already too late. Before she could even see who was behind her, someone hooked an arm around her neck. Stripped her gun from her hand.

And whoever it was put a gun to her head.

HELL. THE GUNMAN wasn't down.

Landon didn't know how the guy had managed to stay on his feet, not after Landon had put two bullets in him. He'd aimed for the guy's chest, figuring he, too, was wearing a vest, but two shots at this close range should have sent the guy to the ground. They didn't.

The man was gasping just as Courtney was doing, but he not only stayed upright but also pulled the trigger. Thank God the shot was off or Landon would have been a dead man.

Another shot came in Landon's direction, and he scrambled to the side. This time when he aimed, he went for the kill. As much as he would have liked to have this guy alive to answer questions, that wasn't going to happen. Landon put two bullets in his head. This time it worked, and the guy didn't manage to get off another shot before he collapsed onto the ground.

Just in case there was some shred of life left in the clown, Landon kicked away the man's weapon. There was no time to check and see if he was truly dead, because he didn't want to stay out of Tessa's line of sight for another second. Plus, he could still hear gunshots just up the street, which meant Grayson and the others were fighting for their lives.

He hurried to Courtney to see how bad her injuries were. There was blood, but from what Landon could tell, the injury was to her shoulder, a part of her that the Kevlar hadn't protected. She would live. Well, she would if she didn't bleed out, and that meant he had to clear the area so they could get her an ambulance.

"Clamp your hand over the wound," he instructed Courtney.

He dragged the wheelchair in front of her so she'd have some cover, and then he turned to check on Tessa.

Landon's heart slammed against his chest.

Tessa was barely visible at the back corner of the building where he'd left her. But she wasn't alone. Landon couldn't see who was with her, but whoever it was had a gun.

"I'm sorry," Tessa said. "I didn't see him in time."

Landon hated that she even felt the need to apologize. With all the bullets flying and the chaos, it would have been hard to hear someone coming up behind her. Besides, they hadn't even known the locations or even the number of the other gunmen. With this guy and the sniper on the roof, there were at least two, but Landon figured there could be others waiting to strike.

For now, though, he had to figure out how to get Tessa away from this goon before one of his comrades showed up to help. To do that, he had to stay alive, so he, too, ducked behind the wheelchair. It was lousy cover, but it was metal and might do the trick. Besides, he didn't plan to be behind cover for long. Not with Tessa in immediate danger.

Even though the timing sucked, Landon thought of what she'd said to him in the car.

I'm in love with you.

Landon hadn't had a chance to react to that, hadn't

even had much time to think about it, but now those words troubled him. Because if Tessa was indeed truly in love with him, she might do anything to try to keep him safe. That might include sacrificing herself.

"I don't know what you want," Landon said to the guy, "but tell me what it'll take for you to release Tessa."

Nothing. For some long heart-pounding moments. Then Landon saw the person lean forward and whisper something in Tessa's ear. He couldn't hear what the guy said, but he got a better look at him. He was wearing a ski mask like the other thugs who'd been trying to kill them.

Not good.

Because it was hard to negotiate with someone who would murder for money.

"He wants Courtney," Tessa relayed. Her voice sounded a lot steadier than Landon figured she actually was. Trying to put on a good front.

Or maybe it was more than that.

She sounded angry. Perhaps because the guy had managed to sneak up on her, or maybe he'd added something else to that whisper.

"Courtney?" Landon questioned. "Why her?"

Landon figured he wasn't going to get a straight answer to that question, and he didn't. In fact, he didn't get an answer at all.

But it did make him think.

All along they'd believed the attacks were about Tessa, about what she possibly saw the night Emmett was murdered. The other theory they'd had was the attacks were connected to him, that Quincy was behind them. But maybe Quincy was after only Courtney and the baby, and Tessa and he just got in the way.

"Quincy's dead," he told the thug in case he hadn't noticed the body. "I hope he paid you in advance or you're out of luck."

The guy whispered something else to Tessa. "He still wants Courtney. He wants you to step aside."

Well, hell. Quincy must have left orders to kill Courtney even if something happened to him.

"If you kill Courtney, you'll make the baby an orphan," Landon tried again. "Whatever Quincy paid you or planned to pay you, I'll give you double. All you have to do is let Tessa go."

Of course, that might just prompt the guy to take her hostage, but every second he had a gun to her head was a second that could take this situation from bad to worse.

And it got worse, all right.

Landon heard the sound of an engine. Not a car. But rather a motorcycle. And it was coming at them fast. It didn't take long for it to come barreling up the alley, and Landon saw yet one more thing he didn't want to see.

Another ski-mask-wearing thug.

He brought the motorcycle to a stop right beside Tessa and his partner in crime. Landon wanted to send a shot right into the guy's head, but the thug holding Tessa might retaliate and do the same to her.

"I can pay you off, too," Landon told the second thug. He practically had to shout to be heard over the motorcycle engine. "With Quincy dead, wouldn't you rather have all that money than end up dead?"

"I got no plans to die," the one on the motorcycle shouted back. He was bulky, the size of a linebacker and armed to the hilt.

He killed the engine and climbed off, and Landon could have sworn his heart skipped some beats when he saw what was happening. The thugs switched places, and the whispering one who was holding Tessa dragged her onto the motorcycle with him.

Hell. Time was up. Landon couldn't let the guy just drive off with Tessa, because he was certain he'd never see her alive again.

"When you're ready to give us Courtney," the bulky guy said, "then you'll get Tessa back."

Landon doubted that. No way would they leave Tessa alive. "Take me instead," Landon bargained.

Tessa frantically shook her head and moved as if ready to cooperate with this stupid plan that would get her killed. Yeah, she'd been right about that *I'm in love with you*. She was putting her life ahead of his, and that wasn't going to happen.

"Lawmen don't make good hostages." The bulky guy again, though the other thug, the whisperer, said something else to Tessa. Something that Landon couldn't catch.

But whatever it was caused Tessa's shoulders to snap back.

"Landon, watch out!" she shouted.

The bulky guy took aim at Landon, and Landon had no choice but to fire.

Chapter Seventeen

The man who still had hold of Tessa yanked her to the side of the motorcycle. Just as the sound of two shots cracked through the air. One of those shots had come from Landon. The other, the thug who'd ridden up on the motorcycle.

Tessa hit the ground, hard, so hard that it knocked the breath out of her, but she fought to get up because she had to stop the big guy from shooting at Landon again. She managed to catch on to his leg, and it off-balanced him just enough to cause his next shot to go up in the air.

Landon's didn't.

His bullet went into the guy's shoulder. It didn't kill him, but it sent him scrambling for cover.

The uninjured gunman didn't do anything to help his partner. He latched on to Tessa's hair, dragging her back in front of him. Once again, she was his human shield, and Landon wouldn't have a clean shot to put an end to this.

"Get down!" she shouted to Landon.

He didn't, but at least he hurried back behind the

wheelchair next to Courtney. Courtney was still moaning in pain. Still bleeding, too, from the looks of it, but at least she was alive. For now. And so was Landon. Tessa needed to do something to make sure it stayed that way.

"I'll go with them," she called out.

"No, you won't!" Landon answered. "They'll kill you."

Almost certainly. Tessa didn't want to die, but at least this way, Landon would be safe, and he would be able to get Courtney to the hospital. Samantha wouldn't be an orphan. Of course, if these men killed her, it wouldn't end the danger to Courtney, Landon or the baby, but maybe Landon could get them all to a safe house before the gunmen could regroup and attack again.

Tessa tried to hold on to that hope, and since she was hoping, she added that she could find a way to escape. Maybe she could do that once they had her wherever they were going to take her. All she would need was some kind of distraction.

The injured thug crawled to his partner and whispered something to him that Tessa didn't catch, but whatever it was, it got her captor moving. He had his left hand fisted in her hair, and with the gun jammed against her temple, he hauled her to her feet, keeping behind her. He then began to back his way to the motorcycle.

"We'll trade Tessa for Courtney," the wounded man shouted out to Landon. "You've got thirty seconds to decide."

Tessa knew that wasn't going to happen. No way would she make a trade like that, even though Courtney immediately tried to sit up. Tessa got so caught up in trying to figure out how to stop this that she nearly missed something.

Something critical.

Why was the wounded man doing all the talking? He was having trouble breathing and couldn't stand, and yet the whispering guy had let him bark out the order for the trade.

Why?

Was it because she might recognize his voice?

Even though her mind was whirling, she tried to recall those whispers, but he'd purposely muffled his voice, and that meant this was likely either Joel or Ward. Too bad the men were about the same height and build, or she would have been able to tell from that.

So Tessa went with a bluff. Except in this case, she figured her bluff had a fifty-fifty chance of succeeding.

"The man holding me is Ward," she shouted.

Bingo.

Even though it'd been a bluff, she knew she was right when she heard him mumble some profanity under his breath. Then he cursed some more, much louder.

Yes, definitely Ward.

This time it was Landon who cursed. "How the hell could you do this? You're supposed to uphold the law, not break it."

"Breaking it pays a lot more than upholding it," Ward answered. "Now, bring Courtney to me, or I start shooting."

"You're going to start shooting no matter what I say or do," Landon countered, but Tessa saw him readjusting his position. Probably so he could take the shot if he got it, but Ward was staying right behind her.

But Ward wasn't staying put, either. He was inching her backward, but Tessa couldn't tell if he was trying to get her on the motorcycle or simply closer to his hired gun. Yes, the guy was injured, but that didn't mean he couldn't kill her.

"Who killed Quincy? You?"

"Possibly. He got in the way. He was here to get Courtney, but I never had any intentions of letting him have her."

"Because you want to kill her yourself," Landon concluded.

"She knows too much."

"About what?" Courtney asked, her breath gusting through the groans of pain.

"You don't really want me to go into that here, do you? Because then I'd have to kill Landon."

"I already know," Landon assured him.

It was a lie, but Tessa could feel the muscles in Ward's arm turn to steel.

"This is about your dirty dealings with Joel," Landon went on. "Both Tessa and Courtney were investigating him, and you believed they were on to you. They weren't, but I was."

Tessa hadn't thought it possible, but Ward's arm stiffened even more. "Joel will turn on you," she said.

"Joel's dead," Ward whispered. "Or soon will be. Before he dies, he'll confess to all of this. Including Courtney's murder. And yours."

She was pretty sure that wasn't a bluff. In fact, Ward had no doubt already arranged for Joel's death, and with Ward's connections in law enforcement, he could indeed set up Joel. Then Ward could walk away a free man with all the money he'd made from his business deals with Joel.

Well, he could walk if Landon, Courtney and she were dead.

That meant no matter what Landon and she did, the bottom line was that Ward would kill them. And he would do that before Landon got a chance to tell anyone else. That meant Tessa had to do something fast.

But what?

She went with the first thing that popped into her head. "Landon, did you record Ward's confession with your phone?" she called out.

"Sure did," Landon answered. She doubted he had, but judging from the way Ward started cursing, he didn't know it was a lie. She could see Landon put his left hand in his pocket. "And I just sent it to Grayson. Now every lawman in Silver Creek knows you're a dirty agent."

A feral sound came from Ward's throat, and Tessa knew he was about to shoot her in the head. She didn't waste a second. She dropped to the ground. Or rather that was what she tried to do, but Ward held on to her hair, yanking it so hard that she couldn't choke back a scream of pain.

Not good.

Because her scream brought Landon to his feet. He bolted toward them, firing a shot at the wounded gunman. Tessa wasn't at the right angle to see where his bullet had gone, but since the gunman didn't return fire, she figured Landon had hit his intended target.

Ward moved his gun, too. Aiming it at Landon. But Tessa rammed her elbow into his stomach. It didn't off-balance him, definitely didn't get him to drop his gun, but he had to re-aim, and that was just enough time for Landon to make it to them.

Landon plowed into them, sending all three of them to the ground.

Tessa felt the jolt go through her entire body, and while she didn't lose her breath this time, Ward's gun whacked against the side of her head. At first she thought it was just from the impact, but he did it again.

The pain exploded in her head.

But even with the pain, she heard Landon curse the man, and he dropped his own gun so he could latch on to Ward's wrist with both hands. It stopped Ward from hitting her again. Stopped him from aiming his gun at either of them, but Ward let go of her hair so he could punch Landon with his left hand. And he just kept on punching and kicking him.

Tessa tried to get out of the fray just so she could find some way to stop Ward, but it was hard to move with the struggle going on. She fought, too, clawing at Ward's face, but the man was in such a rage that she wasn't even sure he felt anything.

However, she did.

Ward backhanded her so hard Tessa could have sworn she saw stars. She fell and landed against the hulking hired gun—and yes, he was dead—but before she could spring back to her feet, Landon and Ward were already in a fierce battle. Landon was punching him, but Ward was bashing his gun against Landon's face.

Mercy, there was already so much blood.

Tessa frantically looked around and spotted the dead guy's gun. She wasn't familiar with the weapon and prayed it didn't go off and hit Landon. Still, it was the only thing she had right now. She scooped it up and tried to aim it at Ward.

But she couldn't.

Ward and Landon were tangled together so that she couldn't risk firing. Someone else had no trouble doing that, though. In the distance she heard a fresh round of gunfire. Grayson, the deputies and that sniper. Maybe she could try to put an end to this so she could help them. Until the area was safe, the ambulance wasn't going to be able to get to Courtney to save her life.

Maybe Landon's, too.

In that moment she hated Ward so much that she

wanted to jump into that fight and punch him. But that wouldn't do Landon any good. He was battling for his life. For Courtney's and her lives, too, and Tessa was powerless to help him.

She waited, praying and watching for any opening where she would have a shot. But then she saw something that caused her breath to vanish.

Ward quit hitting Landon with the gun.

And Ward managed to point it at him.

He fired.

Tessa thought maybe she screamed. She screamed inside her head, anyway, and the scream got louder when Landon dropped back.

Oh, God. Had he been shot?

She'd heard that when some people died, their lives flashed before their eyes, and even though she wasn't dying, it happened to her. Tessa saw everything. Her time with Landon. All the mistakes she'd made. All the chances she'd lost to have a life with him.

Ward could have just taken all of that away. He was trying to make sure he killed Landon. He took aim at him again.

Everything inside her went still. And then the rage came. Even though Landon was still too close to fire, she shot the gun into the ground next to the dead man.

Ward whipped his head in her direction, turning his gun toward her. But Landon reacted faster than

Ward did. Landon lunged at the man, twisting his wrist so that the gun was pointed at Ward's chest.

Ward fired.

Like his hired thugs, Ward was wearing a bulletproof vest, so Tessa expected him to make the same groan of pain that she'd heard from Courtney. But what she heard was a gurgling sound. Because Ward's bullet hadn't gone into his vest but rather his neck.

He was bleeding to death right in front of them.

Tessa didn't care. If fact, she wished him dead after all the hurt and misery he'd caused. Instead, she looked at Landon and was terrified of what she might see.

His face was bloody. So was his left arm.

"The bullet just grazed me," he said.

It looked like more than a graze to her, but at least he wasn't dead or dying.

The relief came so hard and fast that she probably would have dropped to her knees if she hadn't heard Courtney groan again.

"Check on her," Landon instructed. "I'll watch this snake."

Tessa nodded, and she somehow managed to get her feet moving. Though she'd made it only a few steps when she heard Ward speak.

Or rather he laughed.

"You think you got Emmett's killer," he said, his voice not much louder than a whisper. Still, Tessa had no trouble hearing it. "You didn't. He's still on the roof, and he's probably killing more Rylands right now."

And with that, Ward drew the last breath he'd ever take.

Chapter Eighteen

Landon didn't want to be stitched up. Hell, he didn't want to be in the hospital ER. He wanted to be out there with Grayson and the rest of his cousins so they could catch Emmett's killer. At least, he was dead certain he wanted that until he took one look at Tessa.

She was staring at him as if she expected him to keel over at any moment.

He was probably looking at her the same way, though.

She'd already gotten a couple of stitches on her forehead where Ward had hit her with his gun. Half of her face was covered in bruises, and there was way too much worry in her eyes. Of course, none of that worry was for her own injuries. It was for Courtney's and his.

"I'm fine," Landon told her, something he'd already said a couple of times. Judging from the way she was nibbling on her lip, he might have to keep repeating it.

"You were shot. Courtney was shot. And Emmett's killer is still out there."

"The only thing that you left out is that Courtney and I are going to be fine."

The doctor had already told them that. Courtney had lost plenty of blood, but the bullet was a through-and-through, so she wouldn't even need surgery. She'd been admitted to the hospital, though, for a transfusion, and Landon had made sure the security guard was posted outside her door. If that sniper, aka Emmett's killer, managed to get away from Grayson's team, Landon didn't want the snake slithering into the hospital to try to finish off a job for his dead boss.

"Are you going to be fine?" Landon asked Tessa the moment the nurse stepped away from him.

She nodded, but he wondered if that was the biggest lie of the night. This nightmare was going to stay with her for the rest of her life, and it wasn't even over yet.

Landon got up from the examining table, trying not to wince. He pretty much failed at that. It felt as if he'd just gotten his butt kicked, but if he could have pretended he wasn't aching from head to toe, he would have. Each wince caused Tessa to look even more worried.

He shut the door and went to her. Not that he thought they needed the privacy, but his mind was still on that sniper showing up. Or at least it was on the sniper until Tessa leaned in and kissed him.

Gently.

Both of them had busted lips, so anything long and deep would have caused some pain. Even that light touch seemed to cause her to flinch, just a little.

"Sorry," he said.

"Don't be. You saved my life." There were tears in her eyes now.

"You saved mine, too."

And since he wanted to do something to rid her of those tears, he risked the pain and kissed her for real. There probably was some pain involved, but his body must have shut it out. Tessa's, as well. Because the sound she made wasn't one of pain. It was that silky little purr of pleasure.

Landon might have just kept on kissing her if the door hadn't opened and Grayson hadn't walked in. Tessa tried to move away from Landon as if they'd been caught doing something wrong, but Landon kept his arm around her.

"Are all the deputies okay?" Landon immediately asked.

"Everyone's fine. We caught the sniper," Grayson said.

Those six words made Landon feel as if a ten-ton weight had been lifted off his shoulders. And his heart. Even though one of the reserve deputies had been injured, none of his cousins had been hurt in this fiasco, and they had Emmett's killer.

Landon cleared his throat before he spoke. "The sniper's alive?"

Grayson nodded. "And he's talking. His name is Albert Hawkins, a former cop. Once he heard Ward was dead and had fingered him for Emmett's murder, I guess he figured if he talked, it might get him a plea deal with the DA or at least get the death penalty off the table."

Landon wasn't sure he wanted deals to be made with his cousin's killer, but as long as he spent the rest of his life behind bars *and* gave them some answers, then he could accept it. Well, he could accept it as much as he could anything about Emmett's murder. And while he didn't like that a killer would be giving them those answers, the man who'd orchestrated all of this—Ward—was past the point of being able to explain the hellish plan he'd set in motion.

"Did Ward have Emmett murdered because of me?" Landon asked, and he hoped it was an answer he could live with.

Grayson took a moment, probably because this was as hard for him as it was for Landon. "No. It wasn't because of you. Ward sent Hawkins to kidnap Tessa so they could use her to find Courtney. Emmett showed up to talk to Tessa about Joel, and when he tried to stop the kidnapping, Hawkins killed him."

Tessa shuddered, shook her head. "So I'm the reason Emmett was killed."

Landon wanted to nip this in the bud. "No, he died because he was doing what was right." Landon would have done the same thing in Emmett's place. But it might take him a while to convince Tessa that this wasn't her fault.

"I wish I could remember," she whispered.

Landon hoped she didn't get that wish. Judging from Grayson's expression, he felt the same way.

"Hawkins gave you a huge dose of drugs that night," Grayson explained. "He said you were fighting like a wildcat, so he hit you on the head and drugged you and he's the one who put that tracking device in your neck."

Landon gave that some thought. "So the plan was to let her go so that she'd lead him to Courtney?"

Grayson gave another nod.

Landon had to hand it to Ward—it was a plan that could have worked. Even if Tessa had remembered who'd murdered Emmett, she wouldn't have necessarily connected the killer to Ward. Plus, Tessa had the baby with her, so Ward must have believed that Courtney would come for the child.

But something didn't fit.

"Then who put Tessa in the burning barn?" Landon asked.

"Hawkins. On Ward's orders, though. After Tessa didn't lead him to Courtney, Ward figured it was time to cut his losses and get rid of her. He didn't want Tessa coming to any of us for help in case we figured out what was going on. So he used the tracking device to find her, drugged her again and put her in the barn."

"Any idea why he didn't just kill me?" Tessa's voice wasn't exactly steady with that question.

"Again, Ward's orders. He wanted your death to look as if it was connected to Landon. That's why he wrote what he did on the boulder."

It turned Landon's stomach to think about how close Ward had come to making this sick plan work. If Landon hadn't seen the burning barn, he might not have gotten to them in time.

"Hawkins also admitted to putting the note on Emmett's body," Grayson went on. "That was Ward's idea, too, he says. He also says Ward staged those injuries he got and murdered the other guy just so he could leave another of those taunting notes."

It was a good thing Ward was dead, because Landon wanted to pulverize the man for that alone. It'd been torture for Landon to believe he was the reason Emmett had died.

"Please tell me you've arrested Joel for this deadly partnership with Ward," Tessa said. "Or was Ward telling the truth when he said he was going to kill him?"

"No, he's dead, all right. It was set up as a suicide, but I think Ward was tying up loose ends."

And those loose ends included committing more murders tonight. Or rather trying to commit more. It was stupid that so many people had died to cover up a dirty federal agent's crimes.

"The cops did find something interesting near Joel's body," Grayson continued. "Proof of payment for the hit on a man named Harry Schuler."

Landon knew the name, and clearly, so did Tessa. She touched her fingers to her mouth for a moment. "One of the reasons I was investigating Joel," she said, "was because I believed he murdered Schuler."

"And he apparently did," Grayson verified. "I figure Ward had the proof all along and decided to leave it next to Joel's body."

They might never know why Ward had done that. Perhaps to "prove" that Joel had been overcome by guilt from all the illegal things he'd done. But Joel wasn't a man with that kind of a conscience. He might have had no conscience at all.

"So with Joel and Ward dead, the danger is really over," Tessa said. But she didn't sound overjoyed by that as much as just relieved.

"It is," Grayson verified, and he checked the time. "By the way, as soon as we caught Hawkins, I called the safe house and asked them to bring the baby. They should be here soon. I figured Courtney would want to see her daughter."

"She will," Landon agreed.

But Courtney wouldn't just want to see the baby. She would take custody of her. As she should. After all, Courtney was the baby's mother, and she'd been through hell and back to make sure Samantha was safe. Still, Landon felt a pang of a different kind. Not just because they'd all been through this nightmare but because the baby would no longer be part of his life.

Oh, man.

When had that happened?

When had he gone from being married to the badge to missing holding a newborn? For that matter, when had his feelings for Tessa deepened?

And there was no mistaking it—they had deepened. But just how deep were they? Deep, he decided when he glanced at her.

"Are you okay?" Grayson asked him.

Landon didn't want to know what had prompted Grayson to ask that, but he hoped he didn't look as if he'd just been punched in the gut. Though it felt a little like that. A gut punch that made him also feel pretty darn happy.

Grayson tipped his head to Landon's arm, which the nurse had just stitched. "You're sure? You both look beat up."

They were, but Tessa and he nodded. Being beaten up wasn't something Landon wanted to experience again anytime soon, but it could have been a lot worse.

Grayson volleyed glances at both Tessa and Landon and hitched his thumb to the door. "I need to get back to the office. Will you let Courtney know the baby's on the way?"

They assured Grayson that they would, and Tessa and Landon went out into the hall as soon as Grayson walked away. Courtney wasn't far, just a couple of doors away, but Landon had something on his mind, and he didn't want to wait any longer.

"Before all hell broke loose, you told me you were in love with me," Landon said to Tessa.

A quick sigh left her mouth. "I'm sorry about that."

His stomach dropped, and he stopped, caught on to her shoulder. "You're sorry?" And yeah, his tone wasn't a happy one.

"I know how your mind works," she explained. "Hearing that will make you feel obligated in some way, and that's not what I want you to feel."

She would have started walking away if he hadn't held on. He did remember to hold on gently, though, because her shoulders were probably bruised, too.

"What do you want me to feel?" he came out and asked. Except it sounded like an order. So Landon softened his tone and repeated.

And he kissed her, too, just in case she needed any help with that answer.

When he pulled back from the kiss, she was looking at him as if he'd lost his mind. Which was possible. But if so, this was a good kind of mind losing.

She kept staring at him as if trying to gauge his mood or something. So Landon helped her with that, too.

"Tessa, do you want me to be in love with you?"

Still more staring, but her mouth did open a little. "Do you want to be in love with me?" she countered.

Hell. This shouldn't be this hard. He was fumbling the words. Fumbling _this_. So he went with his fallback plan and kissed her again. This time he made it a lot longer, and when he felt her melt against him, Landon thought this might be the time to bare his heart to her.

He was in love with her.

Desperately in love with her.

However, he didn't get out the words before he heard the commotion in the hall. He didn't draw his gun, though, because this commotion was from laughter. He soon saw the source of the laughter when Gage and Kade came into sight. Kade had the baby bundled in his arms.

"Told you," Gage said before they even made it to Landon and Tessa.

Kade chuckled. "Yep." Then Kade glanced at Landon and smiled. "Gage and I were just saying that it wouldn't be long before you two were back together."

"And that caused you to laugh?" Landon asked.

Gage shrugged. "We were just wondering if you'd have that thunderstruck look on your face when you realized you couldn't live without Tessa. You got that look. And Tessa's got that same look about you."

Landon glanced at Tessa, and he frowned. And not because he didn't feel that way about Tessa. He did. But he wasn't especially pleased that his cousins and Tessa had figured this all out before he did. Because Tessa did have that look on her face, and that meant he did, too.

Well, hell.

What now?

Landon got that question answered for him because the baby started to fuss, and besides, Courtney had already waited too long to be with her daughter.

"We can talk about this later," Tessa said, taking Samantha from Kade. Gage dropped kisses on both Tessa's and the baby's cheeks, and his cousins strolled away, still smiling like loons.

Landon gave the baby a cheek kiss, too. His way of saying goodbye. Tessa did the same before they opened the door to the hospital room. Courtney was clearly waiting for them, because the moment she spotted the baby, she got out of the bed. Since she still had an IV in her arm, Landon motioned for her to stay put, and they brought the baby to her.

He could see the love, and relief, all over Courtney's face.

"Thank you," Courtney said, her voice clogged with the emotions. "Grayson had the nurse tell me that the danger was over, but I didn't know I'd get to see Samantha so soon." Tears spilled down her cheeks, but Landon was certain they were happy tears. She tried to blink back some of those tears when she looked at them. "I can't ever thank you enough."

"No," Landon teased, "but you can let us babysit every now and then."

The moment he heard the words leave his mouth, he froze. It was that "us" part. It sounded a lot more than just joint babysitting duties.

And it was.

A lot more.

"I'm in love with you," Landon blurted out, causing both Tessa and Courtney to stare at him.

"I'm guessing you're not talking to me," Courtney joked. She snuggled her baby closer, pressing kisses on her face.

Since Courtney needed some time alone with the baby and since Landon didn't need an audience for the more word fumbling and blurting he was about to do, he gave the baby another kiss. After Tessa had done the same thing and hugged Courtney, Landon led Tessa back into the hall.

"You don't have to tell me that you love me," Tessa tossed out there before he could speak.

"I have to say it because it's true," he argued.

She stared at him as if she might challenge that, so he hauled her to him and kissed her. It was probably a little too rough considering their injuries, but Tessa still made that sound of pleasure.

Landon suddenly wanted to take her somewhere private so he could hear a lot more of those sounds from her.

"Here's how this could work," Landon continued after the kiss had left them both breathless. "We could be sensible about this, and I could just ask you out on a date. One date could lead to a second, third and so on—"

"Or I could just remind you that I'm crazy in love with you, and we could skip the dates and move in together."

He liked the way she was thinking, but Landon wanted more. Heck, he wanted it all.

"We could have lots of sex if I move in with you." She winked, nudged his body with hers.

He liked that way of thinking, too. Really liked it after she gave him another little nudge, but Landon wanted to finish this before his mind got so clouded that he couldn't think.

Landon looked her straight in the eyes. "How long will I have to wait to ask you to marry me?"

Tessa didn't jump to answer, but she did smile.

Then she kissed him. "Two seconds," she said with her mouth against his.

"Too long. Marry me, Tessa."

Landon let her get out the yes before he pulled her back to him for a kiss to seal the deal. This was exactly the *all* that he wanted.

* * * * *

Look for more books in USA TODAY
bestselling author Delores Fossen's miniseries
THE LAWMEN OF SILVER CREEK RANCH,
coming in 2017.

*And don't miss her
brand-new HQN Books trilogy,*
A WRANGLER'S CREEK NOVEL,
beginning in January with
THOSE TEXAS NIGHTS.

*You'll find all of these titles wherever
Harlequin books and ebooks are sold!*

INTRIGUE

Available November 22, 2016

#1677 CARDWELL CHRISTMAS CRIME SCENE
Cardwell Cousins • by B.J. Daniels
Dee Anna Justice doesn't know what to make of private investigator
Beau Tanner and the Cardwell family, who seem ready to welcome her with
open arms. Her convict father says she needs to be protected from a deadly
threat—but can she bring down her walls and let Beau in?

#1678 INVESTIGATING CHRISTMAS
Colby Agency: Family Secrets
by Debra Webb & Regan Black
Lucy Gaines walked away from sexy billionaire Rush Grayson before—the
man who has it all seems to have no capacity for love. But when Lucy's sister
and nephew are kidnapped, Rush is the only one who can save them and
bring her family home for Christmas.

#1679 KANSAS CITY COUNTDOWN
The Precinct: Bachelors in Blue • by Julie Miller
Detective Keir Watson has seventy-two hours to identify the man terrorizing
attorney Kenna Parker. Her amnesia makes identifying her stalker difficult.
But trusting his growing feelings for the older woman? Impossible.

#1680 PHD PROTECTOR
The Men of Search Team Seven • by Cindi Myers
Nuclear scientist Mark Renfro has been kidnapped by a terrorist cell planning
to detonate a nuclear bomb. On the verge of hopelessness, he meets
Erin Daniels, the stepdaughter of his captor, whose life is also on the line.
Only by working together can they escape, and the clock is ticking...

#1681 OVERWHELMING FORCE
Omega Sector: Critical Response • by Janie Crouch
Joe Matarazzo is the best hostage negotiator Omega Sector has ever seen.
But when his ex-lover, lawyer Laura Birchwood, is in a stalker's sights, the
situation may be more than even he can handle.

#1682 MOUNTAIN SHELTER
by Cassie Miles
When an international assassin targets neurosurgeon Jayne Shackleford, it's
up to Dylan Simmons to keep her safe. A bodyguard and tech genius, Dylan
understands Jayne's emotional isolation, and his safe house in the mountains
just might have her letting down her defenses.

REQUEST YOUR FREE BOOKS!
2 FREE NOVELS PLUS 2 FREE GIFTS!

H HARLEQUIN®

INTRIGUE

BREATHTAKING ROMANTIC SUSPENSE

YES! Please send me 2 FREE Harlequin® Intrigue novels and my 2 FREE gifts (gifts are worth about $10). After receiving them, if I don't wish to receive any more books, I can return the shipping statement marked "cancel." If I don't cancel, I will receive 6 brand-new novels every month and be billed just $4.74 per book in the U.S. or $5.49 per book in Canada. That's a savings of at least 12% off the cover price! It's quite a bargain! Shipping and handling is just 50¢ per book in the U.S. and 75¢ per book in Canada.* I understand that accepting the 2 free books and gifts places me under no obligation to buy anything. I can always return a shipment and cancel at any time. Even if I never buy another book, the two free books and gifts are mine to keep forever.

182/382 HDN GH3D

Name _____ (PLEASE PRINT)

Address _____ Apt. #

City _____ State/Prov. _____ Zip/Postal Code

Signature (if under 18, a parent or guardian must sign)

Mail to the **Reader Service:**
IN U.S.A.: P.O. Box 1867, Buffalo, NY 14240-1867
IN CANADA: P.O. Box 609, Fort Erie, Ontario L2A 5X3
**Are you a subscriber to Harlequin® Intrigue books
and want to receive the larger-print edition?
Call 1-800-873-8635 or visit www.ReaderService.com.**

* Terms and prices subject to change without notice. Prices do not include applicable taxes. Sales tax applicable in N.Y. Canadian residents will be charged applicable taxes. Offer not valid in Quebec. This offer is limited to one order per household. Not valid for current subscribers to Harlequin Intrigue books. All orders subject to credit approval. Credit or debit balances in a customer's account(s) may be offset by any other outstanding balance owed by or to the customer. Please allow 4 to 6 weeks for delivery. Offer available while quantities last.

Your Privacy—The Reader Service is committed to protecting your privacy. Our Privacy Policy is available online at www.ReaderService.com or upon request from the Reader Service.

We make a portion of our mailing list available to reputable third parties that offer products we believe may interest you. If you prefer that we not exchange your name with third parties, or if you wish to clarify or modify your communication preferences, please visit us at www.ReaderService.com/consumerchoice or write to us at Reader Service Preference Service, P.O. Box 9062, Buffalo, NY 14240-9062. Include your complete name and address.

HI15

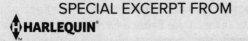
DJ Justice opened the door to her apartment and froze. Nothing looked out of place and yet she took a step back. Her gaze went to the lock. There were scratches around the keyhole. The lock set was one of the first things she'd replaced when she'd rented the apartment.

She eased her hand into the large leather hobo bag that she always carried. Her palm fit smoothly around the grip of the weapon, loaded and ready to fire, as she slowly pushed open the door.

The apartment was small and sparsely furnished. She never stayed anywhere long, so she collected nothing of value that couldn't fit into one suitcase. Spending years on the run as a child, she'd had to leave places in the middle of the night with only minutes to pack.

But that had changed over the past few years. She'd just begun to feel…safe. She liked her job, felt content here. She should have known it couldn't last.

The door creaked open at the touch of her finger, and she quickly scanned the living area. Moving deeper into the apartment, she stepped to the open bathroom door and glanced in. Nothing amiss. At a glance she could see the bathtub, sink and toilet as well as the mirror on the medicine cabinet. The shower door was clear glass. Nothing behind it.

That left just the bedroom. As she stepped soundlessly toward it, she wanted to be wrong. And yet she knew someone had been here. But why break in unless he or she planned to take something?

Or leave something?

Like the time she'd found the bloody hatchet on the fire escape right outside her window when she was eleven. That message had been for her father, the blood from a chicken, he'd told her. Or maybe it hadn't even been blood, he'd said. As if she hadn't seen his fear. As if they hadn't thrown everything they owned into suitcases and escaped in the middle of the night.

She moved to the open bedroom door. The room was small enough that there was sufficient room only for a bed and a simple nightstand with one shelf. The book she'd been reading the night before was on the nightstand, nothing else.

The double bed was made—just as she'd left it.

She started to turn away when she caught a glimmer of something out of the corner of her eye.

EXCLUSIVE
Limited Time Offer

$1.⁰⁰ OFF

New York Times Bestselling Author

B.J. DANIELS

Protecting her life will mean betraying
her trust...

HONOR BOUND

Available October 18, 2016.
Pick up your copy today!

HQN™

$7.99 U.S./$9.99 CAN.

$1.⁰⁰ OFF the purchase price of HONOR BOUND by B.J. Daniels.

Offer valid from October 18, 2016, to November 30, 2016.
Redeemable at participating retail outlets. Not redeemable at Barnes & Noble.
Limit one coupon per purchase. Valid in the U.S.A. and Canada only.

52613975

5 65373 00076 2   (8100)0 12189

® and ™ are trademarks owned and used by the trademark owner and/or its licensee.

© 2016 Harlequin Enterprises Limited

PHCOUPBJD1116

JUST CAN'T GET ENOUGH?

Join our social communities
and talk to us online.

You will have access to the latest
news on upcoming titles and special
promotions, but most importantly,
you can talk to other fans about your
favorite Harlequin reads.

Harlequin.com/Community

 Facebook.com/HarlequinBooks

Twitter.com/HarlequinBooks

Pinterest.com/HarlequinBooks